PLAYING WITH DANGER

EROTIC VAMPIRE PARANOMRAL

SHALA BREECE

plicit Press

CHAPTER 1

"LET ME GO...YOU MONSTER!"

The sound of a young woman wailing in the distance ahead captured our attention.

My dad, who was in the lead, motioned us to quietly follow him as we crept up on the two people.

Without warning, my father aimed and fired the silver arrow directly at the creature attacking the woman in the distance. He immediately freed his victim, who was fled from the scene, terror in her eyes. The vampire turned around to face us, blood dripping down the sides of his jaw.

"Not another step, savage," my father ordered, aiming another arrow at him.

"Lamar, we meet again." The vampire had arrogance in his voice as he flared his fangs at the same time.

Before he could take another step, my father fired another arrow at him, which caught him in the shoulder. I could tell that old age was creeping upon my dad, for he never missed his target.

"Where is Charles, you *cockroach?*

This is the only early mention of Charles. He becomes

the primary antagonist at the end of the story, but we know nothing about him.

"I'm not a sell-out Lamar; you may as well kill me now. I'm not going to give up my master. But don't worry, he'll find you when he's ready. Don't you worry." The vampire let out a roar of loud evil laughter that made me cringe from where I stood.

Although he was weak from the silver arrows that had been pierced through his flesh, he still tried to attack my father. The two men wrestled for a bit, as we watched, ready to jump in the minute my father was in any serious danger. Finally, my father managed to pin him down unto the ground, and as he squeezed onto the vampire's neck, he turned around and called out to me.

"Carrie, toss me the silver dagger!"

I retrieved the weapon and flung it across to my father. He caught it with one hand, while the other hand remained securely in place as he strangled the life out of the vampire. Like a lightning bolt, my father stabbed him in the heart area.

The creature wailed as his body disintegrated into tiny dust-like particles, falling onto the floor.

"Lamar, these creatures are now more ruthless than ever,"

Ethan walked up to my father. Ethan Grey was my father's best friend and right-hand man. These two had been through so much together over the years, that it was almost impossible to imagine life without him.

My father, Lamar Morgan, had been a vampire slayer for over thirty years. Now at the age of twenty-four, I'd spent almost my entire lifetime chasing these deadly immortal beings with him. Whenever we came across a vampire, my father and his group of men made it their duty to destroy the creature and send it back to eternal damnation.

"Why do you hate them so much?" I had asked him one day while I was still a child.

"They don't deserve to co-exist with us humans, darling. You don't understand, vampires get greedy, and like the blood thirsting creatures they are, no matter what they say, they will hunt and kill us humans. So I kill them first."

Once there had been a treaty between vampires and humans that allowed us both to co-exist in the same world, but like my father had said, the vampires grew greedy, and they no longer wanted synthetic blood or animal blood. Most of them wanted pure human blood, from the heart of a live, healthy human being.

I always looked up to my father. He was a very wise man, with strong family values. He did his best with me after my mother died. Although he never discussed the issues surrounding her death, saying that it was too brutal and if I knew it would scar me for life.

What happened to her mother is never revealed, but brought up several times.

I couldn't help but wonder whether she'd died at the hand of a vampire.

"Benson and his clan are getting stronger by night," Ethan told him, with a weary look on his face. Judas Benson was one of the oldest vampires on Staten Island. I'd never seen him, no one had, except my father a very long time ago, before I was born. But everyone knew who he was; he was the leader of the Benson Vampire clan, the most vicious set of vampires out there. They killed with no remorse or regard for human life.

This character and his clan are never mentioned again. I expected him to become the antagonist of the story, but nothing happened. It would make more sense for this to be Charles, and expand on the character/back story from here.

Today we had gone on our usual rounds at midnight, searching the parks waiting to kill any vampires that crossed our path. "How many for the night, darling?" my father asked me.

I had the responsibility of keeping count of the number of vampires that we killed daily. I never fully understood what good keep count was actually doing, since every five minutes a human was being bitten and turned. But I guess keeping track of these things must have made my father and his men feel like progress was being made. It wasn't that I didn't like the whole "killing the vampires' idea," but most of the time, I felt we were fighting a losing battle. Perhaps this was a new phase of evolution and, as the human race, we were meant to embrace it. Maybe it was a world of vampires in the near future and we weren't supposed to fight our fate. I never told my father of these thoughts however, he would never forgive me for having such a thought. He was determined to prove that once the vampire king was slaughtered then all his children would be destroyed.

"Let's go, Carrie," Mason walked over to me, taking my hand in his.

"Let go of me, Mason," I scolded him.

Mason was the arrogant one in the group. For some reason, my father had led him to believe that one day, the two of us would be a couple. But I knew that this would only happen over my dead body. Mason was an arrogant jerk that I wanted nothing to do with. Just the way he smirked at me made me cringe in disgust.

"You and I will NEVER happen. Okay?" I always tried

to establish it in his mind that we would not be together when he got too close to me.

"Keep thinking that, baby," he blew me a kiss.

"Asshole," I blurted out.

"Hey watch your tongue," he shot at me. "Lamar, see what I'm talking about," he said to my father.

"Yeah, yeah, just give her some time, she can be a bit of a shrew," my father encouraged.

"Dad...stop it..." I whined.

We continued walking out of the park back to our car. As we drove around, occasionally we spotted a vampire attached and stopped to kill the vampire or vampires. I always enjoyed seeing the look on their faces when they saw my father; he was like a nightmare to most of the vampires. Some even tried to run away when they came into contact with him. But he never let them escape, never.

I had picked up a few tricks and tactics from my father. I was an expert with a knife; I wasn't as good with a gun. I could handle my own, but if I came in contact with a vampire...

When we made it to the loft where we stayed, my father, Ethan, Mason, and the other three men in our crew went to the drawing board and planned where they would go tomorrow and what they would do in their fight against the vampires. I went to bed. Although I admired what my father did, I wasn't certain that I wanted to spend the rest of my life like him; bitter and unhappy with one thing on my mind, killing vampires.

The following day, I decided to go to a local bar to get a few drinks while the men were back at the loft playing poker. As I stepped into the bar, I got an eerie feeling. In the corner of my eye, I could see several people focusing their gazes upon me.

Could it be what I was thinking? Were they all vampires? No – it can't be, I assured myself, vampires didn't come out during the day. They were all nightwalkers.

"Hello, hello...And who do we have here?" A dark-haired middle-aged man approached me. His eyes were as dark as night, and a chill ran through my body. And I knew instantly that he was not a human being.

"Vampire," I sneered at him, trying to reach for my knife tucked between my belt and my tight blue jeans.

"Ah, ah, ah! Aren't you a naughty little girl?" I turned around and another man was forcefully restraining me against my will. In a matter of seconds, a swarm of men had surrounded me. I could smell the scent of fresh human blood on their breaths, these were a set of vicious killers, and they had me cornered. In that brief confrontational moment, I accepted the fact that they would bite me, and turn me into one of their own. And then I would be slain by the hands of my very own father. Such was my fate – and I accepted it.

"Go ahead bite me...I don't fear death," I told them, looking them each in the eye one by one.

"Get away from her!" A voice called out in a distance. Several loud gunshots were fired, and suddenly the vampires around me were being hit with what seemed like silver bullets, killing them instantly.

"Grab my hand!" the stranger extended a hand out to me, as he fired several shots at the vampires who were all trying to get a go at me.

I followed his lead and we both ran out of the bar as fast as we could, with him, turning behind to fire shots are the vampires who tried to trail us. We got to a sleek black sports car parked in the back.

"Get in!" he instructed, and I hopped in without asking

any questions. We drove for miles with him finally pulling up to a deserted house far away from the main road.

"Are you insane trying to surrender to those guys? Aren't you the daughter of that vampire slayer, Lamar something?" He had a bit of anger in his voice as he slammed his door behind him walking toward the house.

"Hey, how do you know me?" I called out to him, running, trying to catch up.

He didn't answer me, but got his keys and put it into the keyhole, turning it clockwise. "Hey, I'm talking to you," I tapped him on the shoulder to get his attention.

"What?" he turned around suddenly and asked in an irate tone of voice.

"How do you know my father? And how do you know me?" I asked again, giving him an intense stare. Little did he know I could be very persistent when I wanted to find out something.

"Listen, sweetheart, everyone knows your father, and everyone knows you by association. Okay? And these guys at the club, they wouldn't have bitten you, they would have KILLED you."

"What! Why?"

"Didn't you hear what I just told you? Everyone knows your father. They would have killed you to get back at him. There's a bounty on your head. And these vampires, if they get you, they will kill you and take you to their boss."

"Oh my God! I need to tell my father about this," I gasped.

"Come on, get inside quickly, we need to get you showered and remove your scent, or they will track you here."

"But what about my dad? I need to tell him," I insisted.

"Listen to me," he gripped my arm firmly, with almost too much force than was needed. "If you go out there tonight, you will die. And I'm not talking about dying and coming back again as a vampire; I'm talking about dying, where they'll send you back in pieces to your father. Okay?"

I looked in horror, as a fearful feeling rushed through my body. I had never been so terrified before. All my life I'd always thought that if I were to die, it would be in the form of me being bitten by a vampire. I never imagined that they'd want to really kill me. I couldn't help it, I could feel the tears welling up in my eyes, and there was nothing I could do to stop it.

"Oh my God!" I sobbed, burying my face into my open palm.

The handsome stranger stood there, speechless for a while. Then I felt his warmness getting closer to me. "Don't cry, it'll be okay," his heart must have cracked seeing me sob. He tried to console me saying that he would drop me off first thing tomorrow morning when the sun was up.

"Alex is that you?" a woman's voice called out, and her footsteps were heard as she came down the flight of stairs.

I knew it; I thought to myself, he was married. I turned around to see a frail older woman, with several strands of grey hair. Her jaw dropped when she says who I was and a look of terror swept across her elderly features.

"Alex!" she hissed. "How dare you bring this woman into my house?"

"It's fine mom, she will be leaving tomorrow. She needed somewhere to stay the night," he informed her, turning to me and smiling sheepishly. That was a first, someone who actually said that they didn't want me in their home, while I was present.

"That's okay, Alex..." I turned around to him. The entire time he'd never told me his name, and I had not tried to find out either. "I can leave, I don't mind, really, I'll be fine."

"NO," he gripped my arm just as I was heading to the door. He turned to his mother and explained how he'd saved my life at the bar, and how the vampires were out to get me because of the bounty on my head. "So you see mom, you'd be sending an innocent girl out to be killed by these pack of wild bloodsuckers."

His mother looked at me pensively as if trying to decide whether she should let me go out to get killed or not. "She can spend the night, but she leaves first thing tomorrow morning," she said giving me a wary look as she walked away.

"Ensure that she takes a shower and she uses some of your cologne or something, I don't want any darn vampires lurking around my house tonight," she called out to him.

"Yes ma'am," he replied.

"Follow me, you need to clean up." It was then I realized that I had blood splatter all over my plaid blouse.

"So what's up with your mom, why does she hate me so much?"

"It's a long story, but don't worry about her, she's actually a very sweet old lady."

"Really, I could tell," I teased.

He laughed. "She's just been through a lot." He opened the door to the bathroom for me. "There comes a time, when you go through so much, that you trust no one." He handed me a clean towel.

"Yeah, I know all about that, trust me," I replied to his statement.

"Well, it's like that for my mom. The only man she ever loved used her until she had nothing more to give, and then he just left."

"I'm sorry," I said stepping behind the somewhat see-through shower curtain. We kept chatting while I undressed privately behind the shower curtain. The more we spoke the more comfortable we were becoming with each other. It was clear that we had some chemistry between us. I didn't believe his story about how he just wandered into the bar full of vampires and saved my life. And for the life of me, I didn't understand what he did for a living. Why was he carrying all those guns? Was he, too, a vampire slayer?

"So what do you do for a living?" I called out to him, as the water cascaded my naked body.

"It's complicated..." he replied.

"How complicated?"

"Too complicated," he laughed. "I fight for justice," he finally added.

"Oh, so you're a cop or something like that?" I asked.

"Well, along those lines." He finally admitted. He quickly changed the subject of the conversation by asking me why I'd chosen to come to the bar all alone.

"Don't you vampire slayers normally travel together?"

"Yeah, but I like to do my own thing sometimes. You know, some me-time?"

"Yep, I know all about that, but with you...Aren't you worried that you might get killed by one of your father's many enemies?"

"Nah, I figure if anybody or vampire has a bone to settle with my dad, they should find him, and settle the score between the two of them. Why do I have to be involved?"

Alex laughed out loud. He was apparently amused by my answer, but it was the truth. This was how I really did feel.

As my shower came to an end, I retrieved the clean towel and wrapped it around my nakedness before stepping out to where Alex stood waiting for me. His eyes lingered on my body, working their way up from my gorgeous long legs to my deep green eyes.

"Wow, you really are as beautiful as they say. It would have been a shame to lose your life to these guys," he said solemnly.

What exactly did he mean, when he said: "as beautiful as they say"? Who was the "they"?

"Really?" I moved in closer to him. I could tell that he was struggling to maintain his composure. My eyes dropped down to below his midsection where a bulge had formed in the crotch of his pants.

"So, why did you save me?" I moved in closer, pleased with myself for the effect that I was having on him.

"Well..." he cleared his throat. "I'm sure you were worth saving," he gave me a wicked little grin, as his eyes lit up.

"Oh, God...I want you so much," he groaned as I captured his lips with a hungry passionate kiss that sent tiny spasms through my entire body. Our bodies rattled the shelves in the quaint little bathroom, causing a little racket.

"Shhh..." he placed his forefinger on his mouth. "My mother is next door," he whispered as he captured my lips again, this time with a slower passion. Our tongues danced together in the ecstasy of the moment as we continued our kiss.

A soft moan escaped my lips as his kisses trailed down to my neck.

"I can't!" he suddenly pulled away.

"What? No, please do," I whispered desperately. The sensations that his passionate kisses had been bringing about were delicious, and I wanted more.

"Is everything all right in there?" A knock came on the

door. It was his mom; all the noise that we'd been making must have woke her up.

"Yes, everything's fine," He called out to her in a husky voice. I gave him a puzzled look. I didn't quite understand why he'd stopped. Perhaps he knew his mom had heard us, I convinced myself. That had to be the reason. There was no other reason; he'd said it himself, and I was beautiful. So why was it he pulled away and tried to resist me? It had to be because of his mother.

Alex waited for his mother to leave before apologizing profusely to me. He crept out of the bathroom, scrutinizing the hallway to ensure that his mother had gone back to bed before inviting me to join him outside.

I crept out, following him to a room, further down the empty hallway. "Wait here; let me get you something to wear." He stepped into a room, which I assumed to be his. He returned shortly, with a t-shirt and a pair of boxer shorts. "Here you can put this on for the night," he handed me the oversized clothes.

I took them and went over to the room, opposite his which he'd shown me. I dropped myself unto the huge king-sized bed covered with white satin sheets. As much as I hated this, I had to admit that I was tired and needed to get some rest. Tomorrow we would get to the bottom of all of this, I convinced myself. As I lay in the bed, gazing at the ceiling, I dozed off into a deep sleep.

Halfway through the night, a cold chill woke me from my sleep. My eyes shot open, and I realized that the window was open. I could see the moon shining brightly outside. It was a full moon. I rose from the bed and walked over to the window to close it shut.

Walking over to the bed, a strange presence in the room

caught my attention. As I turned around, suddenly, I gasped to see Alex standing in the corner of the room.

"Alex, my God, what are you doing here?"

"Just ensuring that all is well, and you're safe," he replied from where he was standing. His hands were folded across his chest, and he seemed so poised and in control that I almost envied him.

He took slow, deadly steps toward me and wrapped his hands around my tiny waist. Suddenly he pulled me in, closer to him, brushing back the loose strand of hair from my forehead.

His lips came crashing down on mine, with so much passion and hunger that I was almost weak in the knees from it all. As his tongue worked its way into my mouth, I kissed him back feverishly. His hand trailed downwards to my huge, bountiful breasts, fondling them through the fabric of the t-shirt that I had on. I wanted to resist him, but his caresses felt so good that there was not an ounce of resistance from me. My juices made their way from the top of my spine all the way down to the core of my womanhood.

"Oh yes!" I cooed as he slid the boxer shorts that I was wearing down to my knees and then to my ankles. I kicked them off, exposing my clean-shaven mound to him.

Before I could do or say anything more, he scooped me up with his strong tattooed arms and carried me over to the bed. I scurried out of the t-shirt in anticipation of him caressing almost every inch of my naked body.

"Alex, oh God," I moaned, as his kisses lingered upon my perky nipples. While he caressed my nipple with his tongue, he massaged the other free nipple between his thumb and index finger, rolling it into hardened peaks.

Tiny jolts of pleasure rocked through my body with each slow seductive stroke of his tongue on my nipples. His kisses didn't end there; he moved to the other nipple and interchanged what he was doing between the two. His tongue lavished the other just as it had done with the one before.

I cried out in ecstatic bliss as he sucked and licked my nipples one by one. Finally, his kisses trailed down toward my stomach and then to my dripping wet pussy. As he flicked his tongue vigorously over and around my clitoris, I let out several loud groans. He gripped onto my legs firmly and hoisted them up, as he plunged his tongue deeper into my sweet core.

"Oh yes! God! Fuck!" I cried out, closing my eyes, while I bucked my hungry, aching pussy against his lips.

Alex didn't mind, he slowly lapped at my juices with his tongue. Waves after wave of pleasure coursed through my entire being. My moans increased as I struggled to maintain control when he began darting his tongue into my slit. In and out his tongue went, while he massaged my throbbing clitoris with his index finger.

My body shook viciously as I tried to grip onto the sheets for support. It was like nothing I'd ever felt in my life before. The sensations that he was bringing upon me were consuming my thoughts and desires. I cried out for more, as my legs wiggled uncontrollably as he worked his tongue from the slit of my pussy to my clitoris. As he gently tugged onto swollen bud, I closed my eyes and cried out. The delirium of it all was almost too much to bear.

He pulled his lips away from my core, and mounted my nakedness, in missionary style. As he captured my lips with his, I tasted my juices on his tongue as he slipped it inside my mouth. His kisses were intense and my body quivered, desperate for more.

I could feel him probing my moist folds with his rock-hard erection. As it pierced through my tight pussy, I shrieked from the pain of it all. I had only had sex once before, a very long time ago. With my way of life, sex and lovemaking was not a priority. Hell – it didn't even seem like much of an option ever since my dad had been trying to force Mason upon me. I couldn't see myself being with Mason, so I'd kept my distance from him, and abstained from sex altogether.

"It feels like this is your first time. It's so tight down there." He stroked the entrance of my slit with his cock.

As he penetrated my hole with his manhood, I gripped onto his shoulders for support. My fingernails dug into his flesh, and he shot me an intense look. It was almost as if he didn't feel the pain of my sharp fingernails piercing through his skin, and if he did, he must have really enjoyed it. He groaned out in ecstasy as he began moving his shaft in and out of my wetness. He buried himself to the hilt inside me with each hard thrust.

"Give it to me," I groaned in a husky voice as he increased the momentum of his thrusts, slamming his shaft into my pussy. The feel of his rock-hard body ramming against mine made the experience even better.

My moans were soon muffled by his lips once again. His kisses were full of life as his cock explored the insides of my wetness relentlessly. Each hard thrust made my body beacon for more. And he was thoroughly enjoying the ride. I could literally feel his shaft making contact with the walls of my pussy with each hard thrust.

"Harder! Uh-huh, don't stop..."

"You don't want me to stop, really...Okay," he increased his momentum yet again. This time, he captured my lips and was kissing me with a harshness that I'd not felt before from him. It was almost as if he was trying to satisfy some deep need.

I moaned out in ecstasy, calling his name as he rammed his cock into my pussy with fury. Each hard thrust made me even more aroused and desperate to feel his juices inside me.

"Fuck!" he closed his eyes as if concentrating on what he was doing. I could see the look on his face. The look of urgency, the need to release.

He supported his body weight with one hand on either side of my head as he withdrew his shaft almost to its head, and then buried himself deep into my wet pussy.

As he continued to service me with a series of long hard thrusts, coupled with shorter quicker thrusts, his panting and breathing became heavier. He sounded like a man running a race. His energy and vigor were definitely commendable. He locked lips with me once again, as he remained inside me, giving me several short quick thrusts. His cock felt so good – so full of life while inside me.

"I'm coming..." I moaned, closing my eyes tightly while bucking my moistness against his manhood. His thrusts became harder and harder, sending my body spiraling over the edge with each thrust.

Finally, he let out a loud prolonged groan, as he slammed into my pussy with full force. His shaft seemed to reach the deepest depth of my core, as he ejaculated inside me. His juices sipped into my slit and at that same time, I too let out a loud moan as I summited my earth-shattering climax. I could barely open my eyes afterward.

The experience had felt so good. Finally, I opened my eyes, to compliment him on his expert-like abilities.

To my surprise, he was gone. I looked around but he was nowhere to be seen. As my eyes dropped down to my body, I realized that the only thing amiss was the sheet that

I used to cover my body with. Looking over to the window, I realized that it was open yet again.

Had I been dreaming? I stood up, confused, and walked over to the window, turning to the corner where I thought I had spotted Alex a few minutes ago. But the space was empty. It appeared like I had been the only one in the room.

My eyes drifted over to the bed. There a few creases in the exact spot where I had been laying down. However, there were no signs that anyone else had been on the bed with me, much less in my room.

"Gosh – that's so weird," I muttered to myself, carefully scrutinizing the room for any clues. But I didn't find any. I was in the room all along. What a dream – I thought to myself, as I lay back in bed. Before long, I had fallen asleep yet again. This time I didn't wake up until the following morning.

CHAPTER 2

A KNOCK on the bedroom door woke me the following morning. As I opened my eyes, I found Alex walking into the room with a tray in his hand.

"I didn't know what you like, so I prepared a little of everything."

I looked down at the tray that featured several breakfast items.

"Thank you," I said, taking the bowl of milk and pouring some of the cereal from the box on the tray into it. "Cereal is fine...I'm really not much of a breakfast person. But thank you."

He smiled.

"You know what they say, "Breakfast is the most important meal of the day," he teased.

Alex informed me that he would be getting assistance from two of his close friends, Sam and Marla, in fighting off the vampires that had surrounded his house. They would be coming to the house shortly.

I didn't quite understand how they would get to the house, since Alex had told me about the vampires that seemed to be all around. If they were all around here, they would surely kill anyone coming in or out of the place. When I mentioned my concern to Alex, he simply said, "Sam and Marla know how to handle themselves. They'll be here before you know it." He began to leave.

"I'm coming with you," I called out to him.

Alex didn't even look at me when he replied, "No you're not, and you need to remain here, where it's safe."

I tried to argue with him as to why I should go with them, but he was not having it. I decided to drop the issue, knowing full well that I would be going out with them.

I got out of bed, and walked out to the window, staring out. I didn't see a living soul, but maybe that was fine since vampires were not part of the living, they were doomed evil creatures. At that moment, I wish I could see my father, to at least warn him.

If they were after me, I was sure they'd be after him. He could fight them, but could he really survive what was coming? A war, as Alex's mom, had plainly stated. My dad was not getting any younger. His fighting skills had been great during his younger days, but now, as he got older, he wouldn't be able to fight off several vampires all at once. Even with the crew that we worked with, I was unsure whether they'd be able to ward off a large group of vampires.

Suddenly I could see something coming in the distance. They were two distinct figures, and they were headed toward the house. They were both dressed in long black cloaks and I called out to Alex, asking him who they were.

"They're earlier than I expected." He left my room and the sound of his footsteps galloping down the stairs let me know was headed to the front door. I watched through the window as he walked out to greet them.

The two men hugged briefly before Alex moved his attention to the woman. He brought her hand to his lips and kissed the back of it lightly. I could tell that these two people were dear to him.

When all three of them began walking toward the front door, I stepped away from the window, fearing that they might see me peering out at them. The knock on the bedroom door came a few minutes later. Alex wanted me to come downstairs to meet his friends.

As we pranced down the winding flight of stairs, the first thing that caught my attention was the smile on the blonde woman's face. She had a pleasantly calm disposure.

"She's beautiful Alex...I'm happy you let us meet her," she said, walking up to me.

I looked over at Alex with a hint of confusion on my face. By the way, the woman spoke, it made me think that she perhaps knew me or knew of me.

Alex laughed her off, ignoring her comment. "Come, did you guys have any trouble getting here?" He gave them an intense stare. His eyes moved from Sam to Marla. The eerie feeling in the room couldn't be explained. It was as if everyone knew exactly how serious the matter was.

I'd helped my dad fight off vampires for years and I was sure I would be an asset in their little clique. Although they had warm, pleasant attitudes, the way they tried to shield me from the outside world almost made me feel like an outcast. They could all be easily killed by these vampires outside, just like me.

"They've been gone for a while because no one stopped us on our way here, but they'll probably be back by nightfall," Sam answered in relation to the question Alex had asked.

I looked over at Sam as he spoke; he was almost as handsome as Alex. He was a tall, good-looking dark-haired man of mixed descent. He had a serious look on his face most of the time. In a way, he was mysteriously seductive. I couldn't tell whether he and Marla was a couple or whether they were just friends. If they were friends, they must have been very close friends. I glanced over at Alex. I immediately forgot that there was another man standing in the room. Alex was drop-dead gorgeous. He was the man of my dreams in every sense of the word.

The three of them headed to the den to make preparations. I wanted to follow them, but the fact that Alex had made it perfectly clear that he didn't want me involved made me decide to give them a little privacy. I plopped myself down on the sofa and waited for what seemed like hours. What were they discussing? Sam emerged out of the den first; he was followed by Alex and then Marla. I left the living room briefly to go upstairs to think about what I should do. I returned to the room to get ready to go with them. When I returned, Marla was standing over by the fireplace with a pensive look on her face. She turned around and shot me a wide smile.

"I've always wondered what it would be like to have such a well-known father," she said.

"It's fine," I laughed. "The only downside is that you make more enemies instead of friends."

"I'm sure it's not as bad as you think, you've got Alex on your side. He'll do whatever it takes to protect you. He's got a good heart."

"Yeah, I could tell."

"He likes you, you know," her voice was low and calm.

"Ladies, getting to know each other I see,"

We both turned our attention to Alex as he walked into the room, Sam walking closely behind him.

"Let's get the stuff Marla," Sam said. Marla nodded her head in acknowledgment. She took several strides across the room, closing in the gap between her and Sam.

"I'm coming with you guys."

"No, you will remain here until we return." Alex's voice was firm.

"I'm not staying here while you guys are out there fighting my battle," I shot back at him.

"Listen to me; I may not even make it back." His voice grew dark and cold. "There's so much more to this story. I don't want you to risk your life out there."

"Don't get me wrong, I'm grateful for all you've done, but I need to be out there with you guys trying to defend myself. Can't you understand that?"

Alex must have realized that my mind was made up and that there was nothing he could do or say that would make me agree to stay at the house.

"Okay fine, but don't do anything stupid."

"Anything stupid? Need I remind you of who I am? I've been doing this my entire life, so you don't need to worry about me doing anything... stupid."

"Okay, good," he said with exasperation lingering upon his deep husky voice.

I had to admit that I may have been a bit of a handful, but it did seem insulting to have him treat me like a six-year-old. All my life, I had done what I want and gone where I want, without anyone thinking that they had such authority to tell me what to do. Even my own father knew that I had a strong spirit, and he didn't try to control me. The more I thought about it, the more I pitied the poor fellow. He knew so little about me. If we were going to be spending time together, he'd have to know that I was not like most women. I was a dominator, never submissive or weak.

"Here, take this, shoot anyone or anything that approaches you, unless it's one of us," Alex said, handing me a black pistol.

I took the weapon and carefully examined it with my eyes. "Silver bullets I suppose?"

"Yes, so don't go wasting them."

"We're ready when you are," Marla's voice called out from the distance.

"Right, let's go." Alex took the lead, grabbing his black trench coat and throwing it over his broad shoulders.

As we walked into the bushes at the side of the house, a familiar feeling returned. It almost felt like all these times I had gone out with my father and his crew had prepared me for this. The moment when I'd have to fight on my own without my father. This was my battle.

The further we went into the woods, the more terrifying it became. It was like a scene from a horror movie, where everyone knows that something terrible was about to happen, but no one knows what or from what angle. However, the weird feeling that someone or something was watching us made me quiver.

There was a sudden gust of wind and loud roaring laughter. "You think you can stop what's about to happen Alex?" A deep voice bellowed. Alex had sharp reflexes, and before I could blink, he'd captured a man by the throat. The pale-looking man snared, and his fangs shot out as the two of them wrestled. There was something mysterious about their hustle. They seemed to have matched strengths. Vampires were much stronger than us human beings. Before I could make a conclusive decision about what was happening between the two men, Marla's voice screamed out to me, "Look out Carrie!" I managed to quickly turn around and stab the creature with my silver dagger. I had always carried this weapon on my person at all times. And today, like several other occasions, having it had just saved my life.

The middle-aged-looking man gave me a cringed look that let me know that he was in pain. I pushed the blunt object deeper into his stomach area and twisted it viciously into his flesh.

"NO!" he wailed in pain as his body disintegrated into thin dust. The blunt silver object piercing through his skin was every vampire's worst nightmare.

I spun around, holding the dagger tightly in my hands as my eyes perused my environment. In the corner of my eyes, I could see two other vampires quickly approaching me from the left. Without hesitation, I reached for the pistol and shot them each several times. The silver bullets pierced their skins as they wailed, dropping down to the ground and dying almost instantly.

The sounds of the fighting going on around me caught my attention. But it was all happening almost too fast. I fired another round of ammunition to ward off two other vampires who apparently had been hiding in the trees above. One disintegrated in mid-air before his body ever made it to the ground, while the other fell to the ground wounded. The bullet had caught him as he was descending. As his body made contact with the ground, he tried to squirm away from me. I took a few deadly steps toward him.

"No, please don't kill me...Spare me, please...I'll leave, you'll never hear from me again," he begged. Although everything in me wanted to kill him, I just couldn't do it.

His pleading eyes melted my heart and in a way, I empathized with him and pitied his poor soul.

"Get out of here, now," I ordered, foolishly thinking that he would just go away. Just as I was turning my back and walking off, he proved what my father had been saying to me all those years – vampires cannot be trusted.

Unbeknownst to me, the bullet had only lightly grazed his right shoulder and he was just pretending to be really hurt. It was all part of his plan to kill me.

"And now I'll kill you like you killed my brother." He aimed a gun at me and got ready to fire it at me.

"Nooo..." Marla's cry caught my attention just as she shoved me out of the way, catching the bullet that was intended for me. Both Marla and I fell to the ground and it was only then I realized the man on the ground had tried to kill me just seconds after I had spared his life, and that Marla had lovingly sacrificed hers for mine.

"You killed my brother and now I'll kill you the same way, wretched human!" He aimed his gun at me as I held a dying Marla in my arms on the ground. I closed my eyes in anticipation of the fatal shot. But it never happened. As I opened my eyes slowly, I realized the awkward expression on his face. His body then split in half from his head down. Behind him stood Sam, who was holding a long, blood-drenched samurai sword in his hand. He'd been the one to deliver the deadly blow to the man.

"Sam...." Marla's voice was fading as she coughed up some blood. I looked in horror upon realizing that her blood was dark red – just like the blood of the vampires.

"You're one of them?" I asked in shock, my tone sounding like broken glass to my own ears.

"Yes...But I never wanted..." She coughed up some more blood. "I never wanted this curse..." She added as her eyes went still. The other vampire had shot her with a silver bullet and so she had practically no chance of survival.

Sam rushed over, taking her lifeless body in his arms as his eyes filled with tears upon the realization that she was dead.

"Leave now, Sam. Take Carrie with you!" Alex ordered.

"No! I'm not leaving you here alone."

"NOW SAM," he yelled in a loud and thunderous voice.

Without further hesitation, Sam walked over to me clenching Marla in his arms and ordered me to come with him.

I was unsure whether he too was a vampire, but I didn't mention it. I rose to my feet.

"Run! Hurry! Go!" Alex bellowed as he fought off a ring of vampires that had surrounded him with a long samurai sword similar to Sam's sword.

I took off with Sam, running as fast as I could. Several other vampires tried to stop us along the way but both Sam and I fought them off. Before long Marla's body disintegrated and turned to dust just like all the other vampires that had died. Sam crashed his teeth crying out with grief. He too sacrificed himself for me. It was then I realized that he was a mortal like me.

Sections like this pop up throughout the story – very rushed, non-explained events that have an impact on the story. Sam goes from carrying Marla's dead body to dead one sentence later; there should be at least a brief explanation as to how he died.

His last word to me was "Run!"

I brushed back my tears and ran as fast as I could shoot at anything who tried to stop me. I was running and crying at the same time. Within a short space of time, two people had sacrificed themselves for me.

I bumped into something white while I was running. As I looked in fear, Alex's warm smile soothed me. Alex had found me.

"They're both dead Alex," I sobbed, burying my face to his chest. Alex assured me that everything would work out, that I had nothing to worry about. He tried to cheer me up. And as much as I hated to admit it, he was doing an excellent job. I hadn't even known he had a great sense of humor. He left me for the evening, promising to return. I watched as the door closed slowly behind him. "No more crying," I coached myself. Why was I so emotional about the situation?

I dropped down onto the bed and sobbed bitterly, burying my face in the pillow. Everyone around me was suddenly dying. The worst part of it all was I was far from home and missing my father terribly. I hadn't even noticed how much I had been crying. When the door opened, I was startled.

"Are you okay, Carrie?" Alex stood at the door, strong, tall and handsome. He took several steps across the hardwood floor and made his way over to me. I buried my head in the pillow that was before me and tried to muffle my cries. His hot breath on my back of my neck was sweet and almost intoxicating.

I drew my head out of the pillow and looked over at him. He gave me the same look that he had while we'd been in the bathroom.

I rolled over to my back and wrapped my arms around his neck bringing his body closer as his body fell on the bed next to me, his lips came crashing down on mine with much urgency. This time our kiss didn't seem like it would ever end. Wave after wave of pleasure coursed through my body as his tongue probed the insides of my mouth.

A soft moan escaped my lips as he carefully unwrapped the towel that had been wrapped around my body, exposing my complete nakedness to him.

"You have gorgeous breasts, did you know that?" He brought his lips to one of my breasts and teased my nipple lightly with his tongue, before sweeping it up with his hungry mouth, sucking it hard.

"Oh God, yes!" I moaned out breathlessly. His lips moved delightfully from one nipple to the next, bringing about an unimaginable amount of pleasure upon me. He sucked my nipples until they were two hardened peaks. Finally, he released them from his warm lips and worked his way downward to my temple of delight.

When he found my heated core with his wicked little tongue, I wanted to scream out in ecstasy. I groaned as he stroked my moist tender flesh with his tongue, lapping at my sweet juices while probing the insides of my slit with long fingers. I could feel his body stiffening, as he increased my pleasure.

Another series of soft moans escaped my lips, as he wrapped his tongue over and around my swollen nub, sucking it hard, and gently tugging it occasionally. My legs jerked as I bit into the pillow in an effort to muffle my ecstatic cries and my heavy breathing. His tongue made me almost lose control, as I closed my eyes and gave in to the sweet sensations.

"Don't stop, please," I begged, as he elevated my legs on the bed, diving deeper into my core with his tongue. My juices oozed out.

"Fuck! Alex! Oh, yes!" I knotted my finger in his thick silky black hair pushing him harder against my pussy. His kisses became wilder as his licking became more feverish; darting his tongue into my slit with fury. It was almost as if he was searching for some hidden treasure buried deep down inside my pussy.

He made pleasurable noises as he went along. I closed my eyes tightly and clenched my teeth as I focused all my energy on my impending orgasm, bucking my pussy against his lips before finally exploding onto his waiting tongue. He made loud slurping noises as he lapped at my juices.

I took a deep breath and tried to calm down from it all, but Alex didn't stop there, he seemed to be just getting started. "Wait, now let me," I grabbed his crotch and slowly undid his zipper while locking gazes with him.

My hands searched the crack of his zipper and soon found his throbbing manhood. We quickly changed positions, to where he was now laying on the bed on his back and I was the bottom positioned between his legs.

"Gosh – this has to be the biggest cock I've ever seen," I thought, as I slowly caressed his shaft with my hands. As I stroked his erection, I could see the huge bulging veins running across it, all the way up to the top of his shaft.

"Do you like what you see?" he asked with a little smirk on his face.

That coy little devil, he knew he was well endowed. I took him into my mouth again and began working my tongue up and down his full length taking him into my mouth repeatedly and sucking hard, from the bottom all the way up to the head of his shaft.

Using my hand, I maintained control of his shaft by gripping it to the bottom and sucking it hard. His hand went to the back of my head and guided my actions, helping my lips move up and down his throbbing erecting. The more I caressed his shaft, the more I wanted to feel him inside me.

He suddenly pulled my lips off of him and brought my lips up to meet his. I was somewhat surprised by his strength. He seemed to be really, really strong. His kiss was passionate yet very demanding and I groaned as he kissed me deeply.

"Get on it," he instructed, stroking his cock in his hand. "I won't be able to handle being on top."

It was my pleasure to get on top. As I straddled him, his huge shaft penetrated my heated core and he buried himself to the hilt inside my temple of delight, with a hard upwards thrust. His raw meat felt incredible and full of life. As he went up inside me, his huge erection seemed to stretch my pussy to its limit.

I cried out in ecstasy, but my cry was cut short by Alex's lips; he had captured my lips with his passionate kiss. I worked my wet pussy on his shaft, rotating my hips as I went along. He went wild, yanking my hair and forcing my body to arch backward as I rode his shaft.

"Oh, Carrie," he groaned his voice deep and husky and he increased the momentum of his upward thrusts. He was almost like a caged beast that had been released. I wanted nothing more than to pleasure him, more than he'd ever been pleasured before.

"Yes! Yes! God, yes!" I moaned out as he rammed his shaft upward into my temple of delight.

Each hard upward thrust sent my body spiraling over the edge, and I could tell that my orgasm was fast approaching. My juices trickled down my spine and came crashing down below in the core of my womanhood. He was enjoying the feel of my wetness on his shaft because he kept complimenting me on how aroused I was. He pulled me off him and asked me to get on all fours.

With him behind me, he slowly worked his way to my

wet pussy, first using his fingers to stroke my swollen bud lightly from behind before finally penetrating my tenderness with his massive shaft.

"God this feels good," he whispered to himself with delight as he began thrusting his cock into my invitingly warm pussy from behind. His body made contact with my firmly rounded bum with each hard thrust.

"Oh yeah!" I moaned, as he grabbed onto my ass and increased the momentum of his thrusts, launching his cock into my slit with fury. Over and over, he penetrated my tightness, burying himself to the hilt into my moist heat. His grip on my ass got tighter as he began slamming hard against my ass, serving me with several long hard thrusts.

I buried my face into the pillow and bit it hard to keep from crying out. His huge erection felt like it was ripping my pussy from the inside out. Each thrust seemed to be more powerful than the one before. As he increased his momentum, his panting became heavier and I could tell that he was about to climax. With mighty thrusts, he exploded his sea of hot cum inside me. I too let out a loud moan as I reached my earth-shattering climax.

Tiny spasms shot through my entire body, as he slipped his semi-erect shaft from my pussy slowly. The mixture of our cum dripped to the bed. I could literally feel his warm liquid slipping down my tender folds.

"Wow, that was amazing," he complimented as he laid down beside me on the huge king-sized bed.

"I enjoyed every minute of it," I smiled.

Alex leaned over and planted a soft kiss on my forehead. There was something about him that let me know that perhaps he really did care about me, although I couldn't really point my finger on exactly what it was. Maybe it was because of the compassionate stares that he gave me, or the way he caressed my body, and brought me to a great climax. I didn't know, but I was beginning to really enjoy Alex's company.

We remained cuddled in the bed. His lean muscular body keeping mine safe and warm. Alex was a strikingly good-looking fellow. He had dark brown hair with the most beautiful dreamy eyes I'd ever seen. He had a beautiful smile that radiated from deep within his soul. He could melt the heart of even a dragon with his warm smile. His manly scent enthralled me as we both drifted into a deep sleep. When I woke the following morning, I stretched my hand over to him, but the spot in the bed where he'd been laying was bare.

I sprung out of bed suddenly. Had I just made a huge mistake? My eyes caught him standing at the window, viewing out into the bushes up ahead, and a short distance from his home.

"Good morning." I got out of bed, wrapping the sheet around me. I walked over to him and embraced him from behind. For some reason, I was very comfortable around him, and I didn't even think before making contact with him again this morning.

"Good morning to you, too, beautiful," he turned around and kissed me on my forehead lightly. I was very relieved that he seemed to reciprocate my feelings toward him.

"What's wrong?" I asked upon seeing the weary look on his face.

"They're coming; I can sense them from miles away," he warned.

"Oh my God, not again," I whined.

"Don't worry; they can't come near this old house," he assured me with a smile.

"Why? What's up with this house?" I asked curiously.

"It's a long story. But most ordinary vampires can't get inside the house. In here, you're safe. It's out there, and I'm worried about." He gashed his teeth.

A knock came on the door, and soon the old woman I had met yesterday walked in. "Did you tell her Alex?"

Today she seemed more relaxed, almost as if I didn't bother her. She even gave me what I took to be a faint little smile.

"I was just about to." He motioned to her to give us some privacy.

"Tell me what?" I gave him a curious look.

He paused before finally answering. "You may need to stay here with us for the next few days until it's safe to let you leave.

"Oh NO! I can't! My dad will be worried sick."

He gave me a wary look that made me almost want to swallow my words. "Which do you think your dad would rather have: a daughter in hiding who's alive and well, or a dead daughter?"

I thought about what he'd just said for a few minutes.

"Well if you put it like that, I guess, I'll have to wait then." It wasn't that I didn't want to spend time with Alex, it's just that I knew my father, and he'd probably think I was kidnapped or something.

"Okay how about I do this. I'll send him a message to let him know you're fine. How does that sound?"

"Thank you." I went on the tip of my toes and brought my lips to meet his, kissing him lightly, to show him my gratitude and appreciation.

CHAPTER 3

A FEW DAYS went by as I stayed with Alex and his family. The relationship between his mother and I had become a little more amicable. Today we were in the kitchen preparing lunch when his mother left the kitchen and went upstairs. I continued to work.

The sudden new presence in the kitchen hovering behind me caught my attention. I turned around to find Alex standing behind me.

"I got you this," he said as he handed me a handful of strawberries.

"Thank you." I took the fruits and brought them close to my nose, inhaling deeply. Their sweet smell enthralled me. "I'll use them for the pie," I said, giving him a warm smile.

"Strawberry pie used to be my favorite dessert," Alex said, his stare wondering off indicating that it was now all in the past.

I bit into one of the strawberries and indulged. I could see Alex in the corner of my eyes. He had a hungry look on his face. He took a few steps toward me closing the gap between our bodies. Alex had something about him that sent tiny pleasurable tingles through my body whenever he was nearby.

I yelped as he suddenly wrapped his arm around my waist and pulled me in closer. His warm muscular body against mine made me melt in his arms. His lips captured mine with fury as his tongue probed the insides of my mouth with passion. Each kiss sent tiny shockwaves through my body. My hands roamed freely along his huge manly arms.

I felt his body stiffen as my hands dropped down to the buckle of his belt. My body ached for him.

"Whoa, easy there," he pulled away, holding onto my wandering hands. Alex shot me an intense stare. In his eyes, I could see the flames of desire burning brightly. I smiled sheepishly, stroking his almost bare muscular chest.

Alex took a sharp deep breath, closing his eyes as he released the air. "My God, you're making this incredibly difficult for me." His husky voice made me almost weak in the knees.

I looked up at him. He captured my lips once again, this time his kisses were much more passionate than before. When we broke off his kisses, his body pressed up on mine with my back against the wall. His hands worked their way between my inner thighs to my moist heat. As his hand made contact with my saturated cotton panties, he pulled them to the side and slowly stroked my tender folds with his forefinger.

I cooed as he slipped his fingers onto my inviting warm clit. "Oh, God!" I moaned breathlessly. He soon withdrew his finger and penetrated my core yet again.

"Shit!" I cried out taking several quick deep breaths as he rammed his finger relentlessly into my pussy. I bucked my wetness against his finger as he pleasured me beyond belief.

"Do you like that?" he asked in a desire-filled voice. I struggled to find the words to answer him.

"I asked you a question, do you like that?" he asked again stabbing into me with three of his long fingers.

"Yes! Yes! Yes!" I closed my eyes and gave in to his sweet surrender.

Finally, he pulled away and brought his drenched fingers to my lips, instructing me to take his finger into my mouth. "Taste yourself," he said.

I didn't hesitate; I happily obliged, opening my mouth as he let me suck his fingers. They tasted great and I maintained a firm gaze as I worked my tongue along his finger.

"Delicious," I cooed, giving him a warm smile. He brought his hand down to his bulging erection and whipped out his long massive shaft.

His cock looked delicious and my mouth literally watered as I anticipated how pleasurable it would feel to take him into my wanton lips. Dropping down to my knees before him, I cupped his cock in the palm of my hands.

His body shuddered when I took his throbbing manhood into my warm mouth. Alex let out several loud groans as I held onto the base of his shaft and took him into my mouth. His groans grew louder as I focused my attention on the head of his cock. Using my tongue, I licked over and around his sensitive tip.

"Ahhh. Don't stop," he begged, grabbing the back of my head and knotting his fingers in my long silky hair. He soon began thrusting his massive cock into my mouth over and over.

Finally, he pulled away and yanked my feet up against the wall. He tugged my panties to the side exposing my moist folds. I bit my lips as he penetrated my pussy with his cock. The feel of his massive erection working its way upwards into my moist heat was delicious. With one hard thrust, he buried his cock inside me.

Alex withdrew his shaft from my wetness, and without warning, he slammed his cock into my pussy. I shrieked as he gripped my petite waist and began ramming his cock into my moist core without mercy. Tiny spasms shot through my pussy as he penetrated and rubbed my clit repeatedly.

As he continued to bury himself in me, his panting became heavier. My juices oozed out of my temple of delight and coated his manhood.

His thrusts became more powerful as he increased his momentum.

"Oh yeah, I'm coming..." he groaned, thrusting harder and harder.

With a loud groan and mighty thrust, he exploded his semen into my pussy. He continued to serve me with long, hard thrusts. His juices mixed with mine as I, too, submitted to my climax. Waves of pleasure came crashing through my body as my juices flowed freely from my insides. We quickly straightened up our clothes, fearing that Alex's mom would walk into the kitchen at any time.

The timer on the oven let me know that the chicken casserole I'd been preparing was ready.

"Oh shit!" I turned around quickly to remove the dish from the oven.

"We will set out to the city tomorrow morning at sunrise. I will secure the surroundings in a while when the sun goes down to ensure that it's safe and nobody is watching us."

"Thank you," I muttered.

"You're welcome. If I don't get back here by nightfall, shoot anyone who comes to the door."

The sound of footsteps approaching alerted us that his mother was near. "My mom will take care of you, if anything."

I could hardly believe my ears. His mother looked so weak, so frail; it was hard to imagine her as my appointed protector. Alex must have sensed my uncertainty about his mother's ability to protect me.

"Don't worry; my mom is a lot stronger than she appears." He smiled as he spoke. With that, he left me in the kitchen and disappeared into the living room area. The sound of him chatting with his mother in the distance caught my attention. I took several slow steps toward the door. For some reason, I wanted to hear exactly what they were discussing.

"I don't think you should go out there alone," his mother said.

"Mother, you know that I can do this alone. Besides, who would I take with me? Both of my friends are dead, remember? I can't take Carrie again...they'd kill her on sight."

"I know, I know," his mother sighed. "Okay, but make sure you're careful out there."

"I will."

He returned to the kitchen with his mother. I was most shocked when she apologized to me for her behavior during our first encounter.

"You see, I knew that a lot of people would be out to get you and I just didn't want to lose my son in the process. Alex is all I have." She sobbed.

Alex embraced her, trying to console her by telling her everything would be okay.

"But like his father, he's very stubborn," she said, brushing back her tears.

This was actually the first time I'd heard them mention his father. Although I was a bit curious as to why they didn't speak about him, I never asked. Perhaps they had a good reason for their reserved attitudes.

"But he's a good man – my boy Alex," she added with pride, patting him on the shoulder lightly.

"I know," I smiled looking over at Alex, who blushed a little. I could tell that he and his mother had a very close relationship. Their bond made me wish my own mother was around. My father barely spoke about his ex-wife, my mother. The only thing he ever told me about her was that she'd died a very long time ago, while I was still a child. He seemed to remember very few things about her. Occasionally he would say stuff like, "you have your mother's smile," or "stop behaving like your mother would." But we'd never had a full conversation about her.

Alex left while his mother joined me at the table for lunch. As we ate, she opened up to me and we spoke about my upbringing and the world around us. She informed me that she was actually from Europe and her family had migrated to the United States over fifty years ago. Alex was born here on Staten Island. He was the greatest accomplishment of her life, she stated. His father had once loved her, but his own greed destroyed their once happy family.

I probed her with questions, which she politely answered as we continued to enjoy each other's company. When I asked her about the house, she smiled. I couldn't help but ask because I needed to know why the vampires couldn't get near the house. What type of protection did it have?

It was then she revealed the shocking truth about the

house. It was actually an old church that had been converted into a home. When she bought the house from the church, the head priest had come to bless it as well.

If that was the case, then I had another burning question. How was Marla able to come near it and even come into the house? She too was a vampire.

"Only the pure in heart can come in. We're all God's children and God forgives us all," she replied.

I gave her an intense stare as confusion lurked upon my face.

"Marla was pure at heart. She'd never bit another human being to feed. She spent her time fighting the wicked amongst us. She even married a human – Sam. It was a secret."

"They were married! Sam and Marla?" I blurted out in shock.

"Yes they were, but they kept it a secret."

"Why?"

"Ah....Marla," she sighed. "Marla loved that man with all her heart and she would die if anyone hurt him because of her."

I took a sip from my orange juice as she continued speaking.

"You know what... you'll be safe here, so don't worry too much about all that other stuff," she ended saying.

"Yeah, I know."

Alex joined us just as we were finishing up our lunch. "I see you two are getting along very well," he smiled.

His smile warmed my heart and I brought my gaze to meet his with a smile of my own.

"Your mom here is quite a delightful woman."

"Now, now, don't get jealous Alex. I was just getting to know Miss Carrie a little better."

"Well good, anyway I'm off to set the traps."

"Be careful son." His mother rose to her feet and planted a soft kiss on his forehead.

"I'll be fine mother," he assured her. He then turned his attention to me. "Carrie, I'll see you shortly."

With that, Alex left us with the promise that he'd return. As I watched him leave, fear gripped my body. I had been there when his two friends lost their lives fighting for me. I couldn't let Alex go out there alone. If anything happened to him, I would never forgive myself. I rushed out after him. Like the previous day, he tried to get me to stay behind but my mind was made up and I was stubborn.

However, this time his mother interrupted us. She pleaded with me to stay behind. He'd be safer alone. If I was there, he'd be distracted, she said. Although I really wanted to go, I couldn't disregard her wishes. And so I figured that it wouldn't hurt to stay at the house with her.

"I'll be back before you know it." With that, Alex left and headed out into the woods nearby.

It was late into the evening when he returned exhausted. I could tell that he'd been fighting from the bloodstains on his hand and clothes. Both his mother and I were indeed relieved to see that he had not been injured.

"Told you I'd be back, didn't I?" he said.

He walked passed me and went upstairs. He returned a while later, completely refreshed and clean. He had taken a shower and now he didn't even look like the man that had walked into the door hours earlier.

I decided to give him some private time with his mother and retreated back into the guestroom. As I lay in the bed watching the ceiling, a feeling of sadness swept through me.

At that moment, I decided that no matter what happened I would go home to my father in the morrow. By

God, no human or vampire would prevent me from seeing him.

The light tapping on the door caught me unexpectedly. "Come in," I said.

Alex walked in; he popped himself on the bed next to me.

"You seem sad, what's wrong?"

Was he insane? Nothing seemed to be going good for me. I was far away from home while several bloodthirsty vampires were all trying to kill me. Of course, I would be sad and terrified. I went on a rant telling him exactly what was on my mind.

"So you see why I can't possibly be happy," I ended.

Alex chucked; apparently, my fear and unhappiness amused him.

"What's so funny?" I shot at him.

"You. Why do you have so little faith? I guess I need to make a believer out of you," he whispered.

As I opened my mouth to respond, his lips touched mine. I forgot about what I was about to say as our lips wrestled together passionately. His kisses were hungry and filled with desire and my body shuddered under the feeling of his warm, muscular body. His tongue explored the insides of my mouth vigorously as my arousal peaked.

My body was becoming somewhat enthralled by Alex, and I could feel my sweet juices slipping down between my tender folds. I wanted nothing more than to have him feel me up with his massive shaft.

I moaned out pleading with him to pleasure me further.

"In good time," he assured me, blowing gentle kisses against my cheeks and then my neck. The feel of him, standing close to me, was all I'd ever wanted, and my aching to be with him became almost unbearable.

There was something about Alex that commanded my sweet surrender. "You're safe with me, you know that..."

"I know." My heart seemed to thud uncontrollably, and I captured his lips nervously. His tongue danced with mine, as his fingers stroked along my tender, lily-white flesh. When his hands dropped down to my bosom, a quick jolt of pleasure shot through my entire being.

Gliding his hand slowly beneath the fabric of my blouse, his eyes locked gazes with mine. He was carefully studying and enjoying my every reaction. "I've missed those," he said as peeled away at my bra and revealed my two hardened peaks.

"You have?" My voice was raspy as I tried to maintain my composure. I was elated at the fact that he seemed to be really attracted to me. At the sight of me, his face would light up and his smile would broaden.

His tongue felt magical as it stroked my nipples, lightly, traveling in small circles before sucking onto it. As he took me into his mouth repeatedly, I cocked my head back and heaved my chest harder against his lips. His tongue moved feverishly, licking and caressing my nipples, focusing on each one with much precision and delicacy.

As he continued his sweet caresses, he slowly helped me ease onto the bed. The soft cotton sheets against my back made the experience all the more pleasurable. My eyes came together and I saw nothing, but only felt the feel of his gentle kisses on my perky nipples. As he increased the momentum of the small circular motions of his tongue, his hands roamed all over the rest of my body. He brought his fingers down to my temple of delight and stroked my moist tender flesh, working his way up from my warm inviting slit to my throbbing clitoris.

"Oh...Don't stop...Please don't stop." I parted my legs

further, allowing him further access into my moist heat. His fingers plunged into my core repeatedly as he served me with several hard thrusts.

"Oh, God!" I squealed, baring my very soul to him.

He finally ended his little torture and stifled my cries of pleasure with his lips, kissing me with so much intensity that I quivered to my core. He broke off his kiss and as I laid there, I could feel his eyes carefully scanning my naked body. In his eyes, he had something dark and mysterious about him. Any other person would probably shy away from Alex, but I didn't. I was not terrified of him; I was rather intrigued by his dark aura.

He brought his lips back to my heated core and slowly stroked my wetness, stopping at my swollen bud, and puckering his lips around it. I bucked my pussy against his tongue, as sensations gripped my body. It felt like the most magical experience of my life. I could feel my climax quickly approaching, and as he continued his sweet caress, I finally gave in. With a loud ecstatic cry, I summited my climax, coating his tongue with my delicious juices.

He helped me simmer down by gently blowing soft kisses against my cum drenched mound. As he changed positions, I brought my fingers to my core, and slid it deep into my slit, bringing it out and up to his lips. "Delicious..." he licked his lips as he took my finger again into his mouth and sucked it lightly.

Tiny spasms shot through my body, as my juices continued to trickle down slowly between my tender flesh. The pulsating pain from the penetration of his massive shaft was like a dagger penetrating my very soul. His raw meat stretched my pussy past its limit to accommodate his thickness and length. My body shuddered as he drove his manhood deeper and deeper into my temple of delight. He eased his body onto mine, supporting his weight by propping himself up with both hands carefully positioned on the bed, one on each side. Slowly he began lowering himself into my wetness, over and over, letting out soft groans as he went about penetrating my core. Each thrust did something to my body, something sweet, something so pleasurable that the only thing I could do was respond by moving my hips in perfect timing with his thrusts.

Deeper and deeper he went with each thrust, burying himself to the hilt inside my warmness.

"You feel so good," he muttered, as he rammed into my pussy repeatedly. His body stiffened, as he increased the momentum. He was now panting heavily, like a man running a race.

"Oh, God! So fucking good!" I cried out in ecstatic bliss. I could feel yet another orgasm on the horizon. He stabbed my insides again with his shaft, forcing me to cry out for more. The feel of his manhood making its way deep down into my sweetness was titillating.

As he continued penetrating my slit with his massive erection, he brought his lips down to mine and kissed me passionately. His kisses intensified my sensations and I tried to transfer as much passion back onto him through my tongue. I closed my eyes and concentrated on finding his tongue as it explored the warm insides of my mouth vigorously.

I could tell that he was getting more and more embroiled in our kisses, and he had little to no control of his body. As his hand traced along the nape of my neck, he tilted it a little to the sides, exposing it to his passion-filled tongue. Just as I braced myself for the feel of his caressing tongue, however, it was not to be. The sharp piercing going through my flesh caught me off guard, and I shrieked at the sudden movement. Alex didn't stop; he continued to pierce through my flesh with what seemed like fangs. It was then in that split moment, a time where I thought my life would be no more, that I realized that Alex was a vampire – a hungry one at that.

I tried to struggle with him, but he was much stronger than I was. It was as if the Alex I knew was no more, his body was controlled by his urges, pure inhuman urges to draw my blood. Almost suddenly, the sharp pain of his fangs sinking into my neck was replaced by an intoxicatingly pleasurable feeling.

I let out a soft moan as he sucked harder, drawing more of my blood from my now almost limp body. When he pulled away, I heard him curse himself remorsefully under his breath. As his eyes dropped down onto my wounded neck, he immediately tried to stop the bleeding. His apologies soon came; he was truly regretful for not being able to control himself some more. He'd just given in to his vampire urges, and he wasn't sure whether I would live or die.

"Alex – how could you?" my voice was weak and crackly, as everything suddenly became a fading haze. I wanted to express just how shocked and upset I was with him, for turning me into one of them – the creature that I'd spent my entire life haunting. But I was too weak, too overcome with hurt to say much. My lips parted as I attempted to utter a few more words to him, but before the words got out, a deep sleep overcame me. As my eyes shut, I saw the shimmering line of tears running down the sides of his cheeks. His wailing was interrupted by a woman's voice, which seemed to chastise him for his actions. It must have been his mother. She must have heard the commotion, my screaming, and probably rushed in to see what was wrong. I lay there, as the sounds of their two voices arguing slowly drifted off.

A gust of wind brushed against my flesh, and my eyes instinctively shot open. Where was I? Was I dead, or was I still alive? As my eyes perused my new environment, I took in the site of the open meadow, as the warm sun kissed my somewhat bare skin. It was then I realized that I was half-naked, with only a white sheet wrapped around my body. My eyes caught on to the figure in the distance. It was a familiar shadow – a man walking toward me. The smell of the fresh summer air, coupled with the feeling of tranquility, made this moment feel like a dream.

"Alex!" I gasped, as the figure in the distance came into full view. As our eyes met, he gave me a loving smile.

"You bastard! Why would you do this to me? How could you not tell me you were a vampire?" The sadness and the hurt that I felt was like nothing I'd felt before. To me, this seemed like the ultimate betrayal. The entire time we'd been fighting off the vampires, he'd been one of them. I just didn't understand why he'd keep such an important piece of information from me.

"I'm sorry, I should have told you," he admitted without trying to argue. He couldn't even look me in the eye, as he spoke. "But I didn't want you to judge me because of this, I never wanted this for you…I care about you deeply Carrie."

His apology seemed sincere but the act that he'd done seemed so malicious that it was hard to get over. Forgiveness was something that I didn't think I'd have for him. Although we'd only spent a few days together, a bond like none other had been formed between Alex and I. It almost seemed like we were too old souls who'd found each other. Until now, I'd thought that Alex and I had been lovers at first sight. But his actions made me think that perhaps he'd staged everything.

"So was this part of your plan?" I gave him a sinister look.

"My plan?" his voice was laced with confusion as his eyes screamed sarcasm in them.

"Don't play dumb with me. I get it; you turn me into a vampire to get back at my dad. What did he do to you, Alex? Did he kill your dad or your brother?"

Alex stood there, speechless. His eyes shifted from me to the field of daisies ahead. He must have had an ulterior motive for biting me, I was sure of it.

"Answer me, Alex!" I bellowed, in an irate voice. His quiet disposition was nerve-wrecking. I needed him to tell me the truth. To explain to me why he just didn't let the other vampires kill me at the bar.

"Listen to me..." he said, shaking me up a bit to get my attention.

"NO! You have nothing to say to me – NOTHING!"

Alex had a startled look on his face. I had never spoken to him in such a harsh tone. As he stood there, his look suddenly became more and more relaxed as a wicked little smile crept upon his face. His lips curled up as his eyes lit up with need in them. He was becoming aroused by my dominating attitude.

"Well think of it like this then...Why would I woo you into coming to stay with me, and then go out to fight for you? Remember? I lost my two friends fighting for you. Surely, you remember that. Don't you?"

Just as I got ready to rebut his statement, his lips captured mine. I tried to push him away at first, but I eventually gave in, allowing him to kiss me even harder than before. He scooped me in his strong manly arms and laid me on the ground in the soft green grass. As I looked up, the clear, calm blue sky soothed me as he gently unwrapped my body from the restriction of the fabric sheet.

"Now I can really enjoy you, as I desire." He planted a soft kiss on my temple as he stroked the length of my nakedness with his long fingers.

Tiny electric sensations shot through my entire being. I let out several soft moans as he increased my pleasure by gently fondling my bountiful breasts. His hands kneaded my full breasts together, as my chest heaved up and down to the feel of his gentle touch.

As he tugged on my hardened nipples lightly, I closed my eyes and let out several sharp cries. He continued to increase my pleasure by blowing soft kisses onto my tenderness. His lips soon trailed down to my temple of delight.

"Oh yes!" I moaned, as his tongue stroked my moist tenderness briefly. Soon he was lapping at my juices, while his fingers penetrated my slit with fury. His long fingers stroked my wetness and made my body almost spiral out of control.

"Do you want this?" he suddenly asked breaking away from what he was doing.

I could hardly believe my ears...he couldn't be serious. At first, I had been upset with him, but now I was too drawn in, and I wanted his everything.

With assurance in my voice and a pleasant smile on my face, I answered his question. "Yes, I want this...I want all of it."

This was exactly what he needed to hear. He immediately brought his lips to mine and captured mine with passion. As our tongues danced together in ecstasy as he brought his shaft to the slit of my pussy. Without warning, he penetrated my core, driving his shaft deep down into my warmness.

He began moving in and out of my wetness, kissing me as he went along. Our sensations were magnified, by the intensity of our kisses. Over and over, he served me with a series of long hard thrusts coupled with shorter quicker thrusts.

"I'm coming...," he groaned, exerting more energy than before. With a hard powerful thrust and loud groan, he buried himself to the hilt. As Alex exploded his sea of hot juices within me, I too summited my earth-shattering climax.

Our juices collided as the delirium of it all rocked our bodies with passion. His body collapsed onto the ground beside me. The smell of the green grass, and the crisp clean air, made the aftermath of our climax all the more enjoyable. I rolled over to my side, locking gazes with him. I tried to be upset for letting myself give in to his sweet caresses, but the more I thought about it, the more I realized that he didn't mean to hurt me. In fact, he'd just been too weak to prevent himself from biting me that evening. Whatever he was, I didn't care. I loved him, and that was all that mattered.

Just as I drifted off into a deep sleep, I awoke in a dark room. In the corner of the room, Alex sat watching me. "You're finally up." He smiled and rose to his feet, moving closer to me.

CHAPTER 4

AS WE DROVE along the lonely, dark street, I could see my house in the distance. It looked like the light at the end of a dark tunnel to me. The house was well lit up, each room glowing. It reminded me of the beautiful pink and white dollhouse that I'd had as a child. The only difference between my dollhouse and my imaginary house was their size.

As we drew nearer, I began wondering how I would deliver the news to my father; the news that I was now a vampire. My heart raced as fear gripped my entire body. I quivered from deep within and I felt like I wanted to crawl into a deep dark hole. I tried to convince myself that my father loved me dearly and that he would accept me in his life, no matter what. It shouldn't matter whether I was a human or a vampire. A small voice in the back of my mind came up with a brilliant plan. Perhaps I should write my father a note, and tell him the truth that way instead.

What if my father was sick and his dying wish was to see me, his precious daughter? If anything happened to him before we could be reunited, I would be furious with myself. My father would be even more furious, with me; I was now a vampire and didn't even bother to tell him in person. He would feel hurt and insulted if I told him via a note. After thinking about it, I decided that it would be best to tell him in person.

However, the question remained, how would I tell him that I was now one of the creatures that he haunted?

Knowing my father's hatred of vampires, I figured that if I were to tell him the truth, he would literally kill me. I had become his enemy, the very thing he hated. Nothing could ease my troubled mind, not even Alex's comforting words. I knew my father and I knew he would probably turn me away once he found out. What would his colleagues say? They, too, hated vampires. How would I ever be able to look them in the eye? I didn't know. The only thing I did know was that I was going to be in serious trouble with my father when he found out.

I decided that if it were possible I would keep this a secret until the time was right to tell him. I looked over at Alex as he focused on steering the car toward the mansion at the end of the winding road. He looked just as handsome as he did the first day I met him. Nothing had changed about him. He was dressed in a blue sweater with a pair of black pants. His dimpled chin and silky hair made him look like John Travolta's brother.

"I hope you come in to meet my father," I said, hoping that if Alex came in, my father's attention would be diverted to him. It would be a step in the right direction to accepting Alex into our family. I was finding myself falling in love with him.

"I don't think that would be such a good idea, he might just have my head," he chuckled lightly. His laughter was as sweet as a child's; it came from his soul. His eyes lit up and amusement danced in them. He was such a sweetheart.

"You never know, I think he'll be nice...You saved my life remember."

"I also ended it with one bite, sweetheart," he interrupted solemnly. It was as if he was filled with remorse. I had forgiven him but he still hadn't forgiven himself for changing me.

"You didn't kill me, Alex. You gave me life, a new, exciting eternal life, and I'm happy." A warm feeling of love was ignited within me, and I knew that I was in love with Alex – the vampire. My gentle words seemed to soothe his worrying mind.

He relaxed and let out a long sigh of relief. Perhaps this was exactly what he needed to hear.

He was almost like a child seeking his mother's approval. I knew that he, too, was a bit fearful. My father was well known. People knew he was ruthless when it came to killing these immortal beings, and Alex knew all too well what he was risking by being in the presence of such a man.

"Don't worry, he'll have to go through me first," I assured him with a smile. I wouldn't let my father hurt him, not in a million years. If things didn't go well I would perhaps sacrifice myself so Alex could escape. But I remained hopeful that both Alex and I would be okay, that my father would never harm me. He loved me, I kept repeating in my mind as if trying to convince myself that we had nothing to fear.

The building was getting closer, and the churning in my stomach grew. I felt like a guilty man about to go into the gas chamber, breathing his final few minutes of life. At that moment I wished I could go back, rewind the past few days, weeks even. But I realized that if the past were to be erased, then I wouldn't have met Alex. I was too in love to want to live life again, with the possibility of never being with Alex.

I could feel the hunger that I'd had before setting out. This hunger had caused Alex and I to feast on the blood of a young deer we'd found running along in the woods. Alex had caught it and snatched the animal's neck off without even thinking twice. When he'd brought it to me, it looked as sumptuous as my favorite dish, the blood hot and rich, with a little sweetness to it. Its flesh I didn't care too much for but I enjoyed the experience nonetheless. Now that it had been hours since I last fed, I was as hungry as a lion trapped in a cage.

"Are you okay?" Alex's voice was laced with concern.

I hesitated before answering his question and he stopped a few inches short of my home. Pulling up on the side of the road, he turned his attention to me.

"What's wrong, sweetheart?" He leaned in closer to me, and I could practically feel his warmth brushing against my pale flesh. He seemed so in tune with me, with how I felt, what I felt. I didn't have to say anything, and he'd just know what to do.

"You're hungry again, aren't you?" he had a pleasant look on his face. "Why didn't you just tell me? I don't want you to starve yourself."

I nodded my head, letting him know that I appreciated everything that he did for me. The dark of the night made it an excellent time to hunt for food. I could see Alex's eyes perusing our environment, in search of something to feed on. Anything with life, anything with the blood, to quench my thirst. I looked away for a second or two, pondering on what to do next.

"I guess I won't be able to keep this from my father," I turned to Alex, but he was gone. My eyes quickly found his figure disappearing into the woods along the roadside. He was moving quickly, just as fast as the flash of lightning that comes before the roaring crack of thunder. He called out to me, asking me to follow his lead. How did he do that? I was beyond that, I wanted to be just like him.

But I followed him, drifting into the woods without my feet making contact with the earth. He brought me to a small town on the other side of the vast tree-filled area. As we roamed the street, three men rushed at us holding knives and a gun. They must have thought of us as naïve strangers. And so they threatened us. "Your money, all of it!" one of them barked out angrily. He hoisted his gun to my temple, showing his intent to shoot me.

I almost burst out laughing when I saw the sinister little grin that Alex had on his face. "Darling, I'd definitely have to say, dinner is served."

The three men looked over at each other, their eyes filled with curiosity. They didn't know or understand what he'd just implied.

"I think I'll enjoy them, thanks, sweetheart," I replied moving closer to the man holding the gun to me. He probably sensed the danger because his hand began shaking. This felt amazing; I could hear the thudding of his heart, and it excited me. At first, he was so brave, so violent, but now, so timid and fear lingered in his eyes. The other two men with him immediately lurched toward Alex, trying their best to struggle with him. But it was as obvious as the light of day; Alex was stronger than the both of them, much, much stronger. With one quick turn and shove, he repelled them both from his body. They fell to the ground with shocked expressions on their faces.

"Wha...Wha...What the hell are you?"

The other two men staggered to their feet. They shot

each other a look and then like two mad dogs they charged toward Alex, aiming their knives at him. But how foolish they were. Alex didn't seem perturbed by the actions; instead, he just stood there waiting. He had a cocky look on his face. Any pity that I had for the men that could have influenced me in sparing their lives was thrown out the window. These lowlifes didn't deserve to live.

Without warning, Alex gave them both a hard, fatal blow with his mighty hand. They flew in the air as if they had been tiny objects picked up in the gusty winds of a tornado. The guy who stood before me looked in horror; he was shaking so hard that the gun he'd been holding fell to the ground.

"Don't be afraid now," I teased, giving the flesh on the nape of his neck a long seductive lick.

I looked over at Alex, who was no longer next to me. He was bent over one of the dead bodies, indulging in the hot pulsating blood that gushed from the man's neck. He looked like a hungry lion feeding on his prey. He looked up as if sensing that I was looking at him, and beckoned me to feast upon the man next to me. Without another word, I sank my fangs into his flesh, sucking long and hard, taking in the sweetness of his hot warm blood. He shrieked in pain, struggling feverishly to escape from me. But I was stronger than he was. I drove my fangs deeper and harder into his neck. I only stopped sucking when his body went limp against me. Satisfied that I had fed sufficiently, I released him. His lifeless body crumbled to the ground.

In that moment, I pitied him a little. Did he really deserve such a death? I almost shed a tear for him, when I felt the warm embrace of Alex take me in from behind. The soft kiss on my neck sent shivers through my body. "It's okay, he won't be missed. You did the world a favor sweetheart," he tried to convince me that killing these men was the best thing. But I just could not justify taking the life of another human. This was my first human killing, and I knew one thing from this experience. I knew that I didn't want to take another life to satisfy my evil thirst. No human deserved to die by my hand or fangs, rather.

"Don't beat yourself up, please...You're feeling like this because it's your first time. Gradually you get better at hunting and you won't feel so bad."

"That's not it, Alex." I wiped back the line of tears that had begun to slowly stream down the sides of my cheeks.

"What is it then?" his voice was laced with concern. He cupped my chin in his hand and hoisted my head so that my gaze met his.

As he looked down into my eyes, I confessed to him, telling him the truth about how I really felt. I was afraid; I didn't want this life if this was the price that I had to pay.

"I just can't do it again, I'm sorry...I'm just not comfortable with killing other people," I sobbed.

"Don't worry; everything's going to be okay," he assured me as if trying to take away my pain.

I smiled and put on a brave face, but deep down inside I wasn't certain that I believed the words that he had just spoken. I didn't see how things would get better. Each day I became stronger, and so did my thirst for blood. Eventually, I figured that I wouldn't be able to control my desires, my urges, for live humans. I would kill myself before I became a vicious man-eating creature that I was sure of.

We drifted back to the cars within a matter of minutes. I looked at myself one last time in the mirror, ensuring that I'd wiped off any blood smears on my face and lips. My dad could sniff a vampire from miles away, and so I had to be extra careful. If he realized that I was a vampire, there was a great possibility that someone could end up dead.

My heart raced frantically as I approached the front door. What would my father say when he saw me? How would he react? A thousand questions seemed to rush through my mind all at the same time. Taking a deep breath in, I knocked again. This time I could hear the footsteps coming toward the door. I swallowed hard, fearing that the man who opened the door would be so upset with me that he would perhaps shut the door in my face. Slowly the knob turned clockwise.

"I've been so worried about you! Where have you been?" My father had a serious look on his face as he spoke.

I took a few steps in, closing the door behind me. He didn't say another word, but stood there, waiting for my answer.

"I'm okay, a few crazy vampires tried to kill me, or whatever, but I was able to escape thanks to the help of a good Samaritan." My father's eyes opened wider and wider as I spoke, showing his dismay.

"Oh honey, I'm so sorry. Thank God you're here now, safe with us." He took a few steps up to me and extended his arms to greet me. I hugged him back, laying my head on his chest. I could hear his heartbeat; it was loud, filled with excitement and content. A strange feeling began to surface; the feeling I'd had a few minutes earlier. A desire, a strong longing to sink my fangs into his delicious flesh, sucking his warm, pulsating blood. I could smell the sweet aroma of his blood, taste it almost. My body ached to have this warm red liquid trickling down my throat, quenching the sinister thirst that was practically driving me near the point of insanity right now.

It was a struggle to pull away from him. He was my

father, and I had to exercise some level of control around him. The last thing I wanted to do was give into my desire and bite him. He loathed vampires so much that if I ever were to bite him, the thought of him turning into a vampire would drive him to commit suicide. He would kill me, and then kill himself.

As we stepped away from each other, my eyes fell in his briefly; I quickly shifted my attention to the painting on the wall. My father's eyes followed mine to the portrait on the wall. "You like it?"

I looked intensely at the two figures in the picture, a father and his daughter, holding hands while walking toward the sunrise, with several other people walking behind them. From what I could see, it appeared that they were leading everyone else to what seemed like a brighter day. Something inside me told me that this was a representation of his feelings toward me; in fact, it was a representation of how he saw his life. Me and him, leading other people toward a brighter future.

"I did it while you were gone. I prayed that you would come back, and I would show it to you. And now here you are looking at it with me." He stopped what he was saying and clasped his hands together, cocking his head up to the ceiling. "Thank you, God, for bringing my daughter back to me."

I stood there, in amazement. In all my years, I'd never seen my father pray before. His actions showed me just how much he really missed me. For a brief moment, I felt bad, ashamed even. My father had done his best to raise me the best way he knew how, yet here I was fighting the urge to bite him.

"I'll go prepare dinner, and then we can talk some more about what happened to you." He marched into the kitchen almost like an angry child who hadn't gotten his way. He meant business. I may not have known everything about my father, but I did know that whenever he was upset or threatened, he acted out. He would just take one of his loaded guns and fire it out into the open. If provoked, he would shoot to kill. The fact that my life was now in danger enraged him. I was certain that he would kill, and search long and hard for those after me.

I walked over to the kitchen behind him. I knew that he was going to prepare one of my favorite dishes. He always prepared lasagna to make me feel better. He knew it was my favorite and so he would always do it for me, and if I was having a bad day, my day would always get better after eating with him.

I grabbed a barstool and sat next to the kitchen counter, watching my father cook as I used to do as a child growing up. He was so organized, laying all his ingredients out on the chopping board, and cutting them in perfect proportions. We engaged in lively conversation as we chatted, reminiscing about the past at times. It seemed like we hadn't seen each other in forever. We had been so busy chatting that we didn't realize how fast the time was flying by. Soon dinner was ready. Although lasagna had been my favorite dish before, I suddenly lost my appetite.

As I sat there, trying to figure out how I would be able to get by without having dinner, my father caught on to me and asked why I had touched on my food yet. I tried to lie but I was not very good at it.

"You love lasagna...I even used my secret ingredient," he tried to coax me into eating. But I didn't. I couldn't imagine the feeling of having food go down my throat right now. Maybe I could pretend to eat it, I thought to myself. After all, this was my favorite dish. And so I tried to fake it.

Pretending to eat my food, while secretly spitting it out into the napkin. My dad didn't seem to notice what I was doing and I was happy.

I rose from my chair and got ready to exit the kitchen when suddenly I felt his hand holding me down. "If there's something bothering you, you know you can share it with me sweetheart," the serious look that he had on his face slowly disappeared and was replaced by a huge smile. Sometimes I forgot how much of a loving dad he had been to me. I know that I didn't have a normal upbringing, but my father did the best he could, given our difficult situation. Not many fathers would have put up with a stubborn young girl, such as me. But my father did, and he hardly complained about it.

"I'm just not feeling too well, Dad, I'm sure I'll feel better tomorrow," I assured him with a smile.

"I don't know, I don't like this little look that you have on your face. I'm worried about you Carrie. Don't shut me out."

"I'm okay dad, it's nothing really. Don't worry; I'll have some more lasagna a bit later on, or tomorrow." With that, I sprung from my seat before he could ask me any more questions.

I knew my father well enough to know that he'd push and push until he got the truth out of me. And I also knew that he couldn't handle the truth, not just yet. I can clearly recall several previous occasions when I would be going through a difficulty and he'd try to help, only becoming upset in the end of it all.

I could hardly wait to get upstairs to the confines of my room; there I'd be safe, and able to think clearly. I had to admit to myself that I felt horrible lying to my father. He would probably understand right off the bat, but no, I chose to keep silent, allowing this deep dark secret to slowly eat up within. As I climbed up the flight of stairs that led to my bedroom, I thought long and hard about what would be the best thing to do. The door to my room was shut. Slowly I opened it and took light steps inside. It felt like I'd been away from it for months.

"Ahhh...," I let out a long sigh as I dropped my body onto my soft cotton sheets that had beautifully covered my queen-sized bed. My eyes perused my room, slowly watching every item within it. Everything seemed to be in place, exactly where I'd left it. Even the bottle of perfume that I'd been wearing the day I'd left to go to the bar was still there, uncovered. I rose from my bed and slowly walked over to the bottle, bringing the tip of it to my nose; I inhaled the all too familiar scent.

Just then, there was a light knock at the door.

"It's me, honey, let me in," my father's voice was heard from behind the door.

"It's open, dad," I called out to him, letting him know that he could just walk in.

"Why is it so dark in here?" I heard him say and before I could reply, he'd switched the lights on. His steps were light as he approached me.

"I couldn't help but notice that there's something different about you. What's wrong, honey?"

There was a long silence in the room, as I searched for the words I could use to explain what had happened to my father. I didn't want to break his heart, but his heart was already breaking from him suspecting that I was keeping something from him.

I tried to brush off his question; saying that my weird behavior was a direct result of me being really exhausted. After a while, he must have realized that he would get nowhere questioning, and so he once again spoke about how much he loved and missed me. "You can come to me to talk about anything honey, anything."

He rose to his feet slowly and gave me one final look. It almost seemed like he was trying to plead with me, one last time, using his eyes. I didn't crack; I tried to maintain my answer that everything was okay.

"Well, I guess we'll chat tomorrow about it." He gave me a faint smile before walking out of my room.

At last, I had the room all to myself, yet again. It was amazing to me how my body had changed; I could hear so much better and my other senses were also heightened. Even now I could hear my father's footsteps pounding on the hardwood floor downstairs. Was this a benefit in disguise? I loved my new senses.

I laid in my bed thinking about what excuse I would use tomorrow as to why I could head out during the day. Alex could, but I couldn't do it. I would literally be set alight by the heat radiating from the sun's rays. Stepping out into the light of day was like vampire suicide.

The more I lay there in bed, the more frustrated I became with myself. There was so much to do, to see outside but yet here I was cooped up in my room. A burning desire was slowly consuming me from the inside out. I wanted to go outside and enjoy the beauty of it all while breathing the warm night air. And so, after a while, after much hesitation on my part, I finally did what I wanted to do. I left and went outside into the night. The nearby woods were pitch dark and I found it warm and inviting. I cruised through the night, stopping to smell the sweetness of the flowers. The more I roamed further into the woods the more alive I became; I was not terrified of anything. In fact, the darkness, and the cold night excited me. The trees were tall, towering to the sky almost and it felt like was in a beautiful dream.

Finally, I made it to the end of the woods and stopped at a small cliff overlooking the main road. I could see the vehicles going by, one by one, as if in intervals. It was a quiet night out, not too much going on, except for the beautiful full moon that seemed to beam brightly from up high. Slowly, I sat down on the bare earth and dug my fingers into it, bringing it up to my nose. Even the earth smelled good. What a cool and relaxing night this had turned out to be. After about an hour of sitting there, I got up and got ready to leave. In the distance, I could hear a young woman's cry piercing through the quiet night.

Immediately I sensed her presence and rushed to her. There, near a river, two young men tried to violate the young girl who fought them viciously, kicking and screaming for help. Without thinking twice, I attacked like a savage beast, ripping them both away from her shivery nakedness. The two young men had a horror-filled look on their flushed faces. One was a bit more terrified than the other. He immediately tried to run away while the other looked on, saying that I didn't know what I'd just gotten myself into.

"Stop!" I gripped him at the collar and slowly hoisted him off the ground; he trembled with fear, as he begged for his life.

I said nothing to him; I just gave him a disgusted little look. In my mind, he was already dead to me, he was a cowardly lowlife. Without uttering a word to him, I tossed him to the side with all my might. His body flung across, making contact with the brick-hard tree bark to my left. I could hear the cracking of his bones, as the force of the impact rocked his entire body. He fell to the ground lifeless.

The other young man, who'd tried to threaten me, was now on his knees pleading for his life. But it was too late for him; his words meant nothing to me. Chances are if I let him go, he'd probably come after the young girl again.

As I approached where he was on his knees, I had a mind to toy with him a little but I decided against it. I would just bite him, and get it over with, drink all his blood and let his dried-up body rot in the forest. And so I did just that.

The screams of the young woman caught my attention soon after; she'd witnessed the entire thing. "GO!" I shot at her, encouraging her to get away from me.

She did, taking off as fast as she could on her two legs.

CHAPTER 5

AS THE DAYS WENT BY, I tried my hardest to keep my deep dark secret away from my father. My days were spent at home, under the pretense that I had caught a nasty flu bug.

"Are you sure you don't want to see a doctor?"

I looked over at my dad and gave him a solemn look. I knew that he was just being persistent because he genuinely had my best interests at heart. He was doing his job as a loving father.

"I'll be fine dad," I gave him a faint smile. In the back of my mind, I knew that I didn't want to continue keeping this from him. It was like a wound that kept hurting me from the inside out, and I needed to just tell the truth. No matter what the outcome would be, I decided that this evening would be the time when I would tell my father the truth. I would let him know that I was a vampire and never lived so freely. I was truly happy and very content with my new life. It was clear to me that perhaps this is what I'd been meant to be all my life.

My dad remained with me for a while before leaving.

He'd mentioned that he had a busy day, and would probably be back late that night. I assured him that I would be
fine. When my father left, I heard his truck pull out of our
drive away. Drifting to the window, I watched as he drove
off, into the early morning sunrise. For the past few days, I
had been researching vampires. I drifted into the study,
where my father had kept several ancient books, and began
browsing through them. I figured that the more I knew
about this, the better it would be living as one.

I kept digging, scanning through volume after volume,
book after book. Soon I found myself reading very old
Romanian texts about vampires. I learned that there once
were vampires who could walk around during the day.
These vampires weren't affected by the sunlight. They were
called an incubus. This must have been why Alex could
walk around in the day and I couldn't. He must have been
an incubus. I continued reading, curious to find out how it
was an incubus came about and if I could become one.

It was late into the morning when I finally found what I
was looking for: a text written sometime around 1602,
author unknown. The book had been translated so many
times over that I wasn't sure what I was reading actually
made sense. I read one passage of text out loud in the darkness of the study:

"They may be among us a narrow section of vampires
with traits not common to those we are familiar with. These
vampires are able to mix with mortals during the daylight
and possess a great amount of strength and wisdom. They
are generally the more peaceful of these beings, living
amongst us as other human beings.

"Younger incubus are said to possess such great strength
that the older males in the vampires often force them into
seclusion for fear of a rebellion. There is a legend of an

uprising so great that it can forever change the world and the lives of both human and non-human beings. This uprising will be led by an incubus, a strong fierce warrior, who will overlook his own desires for the good of all mankind. He will be a traitor to the vampires but a hero to the humans."

I sat back, stunned. Alex was a young incubus who had saved me from the other vampires. Was he this strong warrior that the legend spoke about? It did make some sense; he could walk in the day, and he did tend to be very kind-hearted. I didn't want to jump to any conclusions though and so I tried to finish reading.

However, the rest of the translation was garbled, with references to something that looked like a legendary vampire called The Living Dead. I laughed out loud at that. It sounded like a movie that I'd watched a few months ago. Perhaps this is where they'd gotten the idea from.

After trying to read further, I finally gave up, shaking my head in disbelief. I had spent almost half my day trying to understand this text that wasn't making sense. But on some level, in the back of my mind, I knew that there was something vaguely familiar about what I was reading. It was almost like on some subconscious level it all made sense. But I was too exhausted from my late nights out to be able to stay up during the day. The only thing I wanted at the moment was a long intimate relationship with my bed.

As I lay in my bed, exhausted, I realized just how much I missed Alex. I hadn't heard from or seen him in weeks. I guess he'd stayed away for fear of my father. If my father had seen him hanging around, he would have most probably tried to kill him without asking any questions. Slowly I drifted off into a deep sleep. I dreamt of Alex. I had gone to him. The vivid dream jolted me upright in the bed, panting, and my heart racing. I was seducing Alex, teasing him with my mouth and hands, driving him crazy by bringing him to the edge over and over, withholding myself from him at the last minute, the thing he kept crying out for, the one thing that would send him into ecstasy.

The dream was so real I woke with a throbbing deep inside and the overwhelming need to bring myself to my own orgasm. The memory of sliding Alex's cock into my mouth, of kissing every inch of his beautiful body, seeing him writhing on the bed, begging me to let him fuck me was still with me, the heat and passion still singing in my veins.

I ran both of my hands between my legs, feeling the heat of my own excitement, the wetness of my slit on my fingers. I slid two fingers into myself, thrusting them in and out, and my hips rising and falling in time to my movements. I rubbed my small button, already sensitive and swollen.

I was so excited from the memory of my night with Alex and my dream that it took my only minutes to reach orgasm. With a cry, I arched my back, lifting my hips off the bed, head back, my body convulsing as my orgasm ripped through me.

As I lay there afterward, my heartbeat slowing, breathing returning to normal, I decided it didn't need to stay just a dream. I could really do everything I did to Alex, really experience what I had in my dream and blow his mind along the way. The dream left me believing that Alex was sending me a message, he wanted to see me. I decided that I would go to him; I could play out my little fantasy and see if I really could get him to beg me to let him fuck me.

Without thinking twice, I left my father's house and got on the road to find Alex. Surprisingly I caught up with him sitting outside his house. It seemed like he'd been waiting.

"Alex, my love." I ran to him with arms opened wide.

"Oh Carrie, I've missed you so much." We embraced each other.

Alex confessed that I'd been on his mind all that time. He knew that I would be back one day to be with him and had spent the day in a state of happy anticipation, wanting to see me again, to enjoy my company and the pleasures of my body. There was so much he wanted to show me, he wanted us to enjoy the world as two vampires, experiencing all of the thrills of our heightened senses and capabilities.

As he held me in his arms, his lips captured mine as we kissed passionately, his tongue exploring the insides of my mouth. A wave of pleasure coursed through my body as I enjoyed the warm feeling of my body against his. I was practically vibrating with sexual energy. He broke our kiss, looking down into my face, my cheeks deep red, alight with anticipation.

"You're in a good mood." He smiled, running his finger down my cheek. "Did you have a good day?"

"You have no idea, Alex." I reached up, kissing him again. "No idea at all." He arched an eyebrow at me. "Take me inside, Alex. Take me to your room...to your bed."

Alex did as he was told. We walked into his house; there was no one there, not even his mother. "Where is your mom?" I let my curiosity get the best of me.

Alex explained that she had gone out of town for a few days. "We have the house to ourselves, don't worry," he assured me.

I was almost giddy as we drifted across the floors together, my arm linked through Alex's. He led me upstairs into his room and before he was barely through the door, I was at him, kissing him, pulling at his clothes, and unbuttoning his shirt. He kissed me back, amazed at my aggressive intent on tearing off his clothes.

Alex maneuvered me down to the softness of his bedroom, finally free of all our clothes. Alex looked down at me, amazed again that I was in his arms. He traced his finger down my neck to my breasts, circling one nipple with his finger. My breasts were perfect, full and firm, and the nipples and areola rose pink against my pale skin.

He bent down, running his tongue over that perfect nipple, taking it into his mouth and sucking lustily, pulling hard. He filled his mouth with as much of my breast as he could, lost in the sensations of suckling at my breast.

"Oh, Alex. Oh...that's heaven." I was holding his head, cradling him as he sucked. "You could do that forever and I'd be happy." I felt a jolt of pleasure run through my body as his tongue continued to caress me lightly.

Still sucking my nipple, he ran his hand down my stomach, sliding his fingers between my legs, finding my pussy. I was wet and hot, and I twitched as Alex slid two fingers inside me. He ran his thumb over my clit, feeling it grow hard as he rubbed it. I began thrusting my hips in time to his probing fingers, gasping at the sensations Alex was creating in my body.

I tugged Alex's hair, panting. "Alex, I'm going to come. I don't want to come yet." He reluctantly released my breast, looking dreamily up at me, stilling his probing fingers. I was fluid with pleasure, my eyes luminous in the fading light. He moved up, kissing me deeply.

I pulled Alex over on his back. I reached down, finding his erection, stroking his cock slowly. Alex gasped as my warm hand surrounded him. Slowly I slipped down his chest, licking his nipples, nipping them with my teeth. Alex groaned deep in his chest. "Ahhh..."

"Hush, Alex. Enjoy." I worked my way down his stomach with my mouth, dipping my tongue into his navel, just like my dream. I wanted to torment Alex as long as I could, to drive him crazy, make him beg. I kissed a line down his flat stomach, nibbling and nipping a meandering line across from hip to hip. Alex was flexing his hips in as I gripped firmly onto his sides.

I kissed my way toward Alex's cock, but I continued to stroke him slowly with my hand only, as I licked and kissed the insides of his thighs, tickling the soft skin with my lips. Alex spread his legs, his hips twitching in anticipation. I was patient though and kept working my lips closer to Alex's cock, skimming the base with my lips.

At the first contact with my soft lips, Alex groaned. He reached for me, aching to touch my body. I stayed just out of his reach though, licking and kissing the inside of his thighs, my hot breath on his cock.

"I . . . please." Alex was not above begging; as much as he enjoyed my touch, not being inside me was killing him. I smiled to myself; in my dream, Alex had held out much longer. I took pity on him then.

I straddled Alex, holding his throbbing cock in my hand. I held myself poised above him, watching his face. He grabbed me by the hips, insistently pushing me down toward his aching cock. I relented and lowered myself, feeling his huge erection filling me completely. I closed my eyes, hearing Alex let out a satisfied groan.

Alex began thrusting up into me as I met him halfway, riding his hard cock. When he released my hips and motioned for me to lean forward, I did so without hesitation. He longed to suck my breasts while he fucked me – I could tell from the look in his eyes. I obliged, realizing it was far more exciting letting Alex have his way than it was to make him beg.

Alex was in heaven; his cock was buried in me and his face was buried in my breasts. He sucked and kissed almost frantically as his thrusts became sharper and faster. I was riding him hard; his orgasm was building, heat flooding up the shaft of his cock. I was moaning and crying out for more and he sensed I was close as well.

My orgasm broke suddenly, taking Alex by surprise. He felt warmth flood out of me, my pussy contracting around him. I shuddered against him, my body totally out of my control. Alex held me, held himself still inside me, as my orgasm coursed through my body. My fangs flung out and I wanted to bite him. I realized then how impossible it was to control one's self during an orgasm. I understood why Alex had bit me then. It was a powerful sensation that could not be controlled, regardless of any willpower. As the waves of pleasure coursed through my body, I gave into my desires and sank my fangs deep into his flesh. Alex wailed out in pain but didn't put up a struggle. His blood was sweet as honey, rich, and unlike any other blood, I'd ever tasted. I took in deep draws of his blood, finally pulling away after a few seconds.

"And now we are one, my love," he whispered in my ear as his fingers slowly stroked down the middle of my back.

As I came back to myself, I began moving again, riding Alex as his orgasm built and peaked. He braced his feet on the bed, holding me by my hips as he thrust hard and fast up into me, grunting with each thrust. His cock exploded then, as he cried out, shooting his load into me. It seemed his orgasm was endless; he continued pumping into me, continued shooting his hot cum from his cock as his body twitched and jerked.

As his massive orgasm finally faded, he looked up at me. I was looking down at him, totally enraptured by what I'd just witnessed.

"Wow. That was pretty intense, for both of us." I eased myself off of his cock, sliding down alongside him in the bed. He cradled me against him, too spent to speak. I curled up in his arms and before long, they were both asleep.

As we laid there sleeping I had another dream where he was in it. We were in the white room, light everywhere. He was on the bed, thrusting hard into me, his cock massive and powerful. I was crying out in pleasure beneath him as he pounded into me. He was totally in control of this dream.

"Now, Alex...now!" He bent to my neck, licking the spot below my ear where he intended to bite me again. I tilted my head, giving him full access. He ran his fangs over the skin, breaking the skin, tiny drops of blood a tantalizing taste on his tongue.

He could hold back no longer; he sunk his fangs into my skin, my hot blood spurting into his mouth. I cried out beneath him, convulsing as my orgasm broke over me, intensified by his mouth and teeth on my neck.

Alex's own orgasm broke then, as my blood filled his senses, his cock exploded inside me, almost bending him double with the force of his orgasm and the sensations he was feeling. He sucked deeply and greedily at my neck, filling himself with my blood.

He was blood-drunk, sex-drunk on me, lapping at my neck, his cock still twitching as it pumped the last of his hot load into me. When he finally raised his head, he was looking at a dead white me, completely still beneath him. He panicked, pulling out of me, opening a vein on his wrist, and holding his arm above my mouth. His blood dripped across my parted lips, trickling between them. He saw me swallow and his panic decreased.

I sucked on his arm for a few moments and then pulled him away, rolling onto my side. I was confused; was I remembering the events of the night when Alex had bit me or was I just having a dream? Finally, I willed myself out of this dream, the white room fading, and the bright lights dimming. My vision went black.

I woke slowly, not quite sure where I was. The bed was familiar; I was still in Alex's room. "Good morning, Alex." I smiled, giving him a long lingering look, eyes sliding over his naked body. "You're a mighty fine sight first thing in the morning." I was wearing one of Alex's white dress shirts and as I walked toward Alex, I let the garment fall from my body, standing naked before him.

Alex was in shock. I appeared normal. He wasn't sure what to do or what to expect. As I reached out to touch his chest, he recoiled. "What's the matter, Alex? You look like you've seen a ghost."

"You're not...are you..." He had no idea how to tell me what had happened last night. I had bitten him and drank his blood. "How do you feel?" he asked cautiously.

"I feel wonderful...how should I feel? I had the best night of my life with you." I took another step forward. Alex continued backing away, bumping into the edge of the bed. He sat down hard. Before he could react, I pulled him back and crawled up on the bed, straddling his hips, and pinning him to the bed.

"Alex, what is wrong? Did I do something wrong? Talk to me." There was genuine concern in my eyes. "You're scaring me."

"I, how much do you remember about last night?" Alex was looking up at me, his hand searching his neck for bite marks. I could see two pale red puncture wounds on his lovely neck; he winced when his finger made contact with them. I had bitten him while we made love last night.

"I remember everything, Alex. It was wonderful. I've never felt anything like what I experienced last night, with you. It was magical...everything was magical. Including biting and enjoying the wonderful taste of your blood." I replied, blowing him a soft kiss.

"You know you bit me?" Alex's panic level rose high; I could easily attack him and drink some more of his deliciously rich blood. I wanted to, but I had to control my urges.

"I'm not normal Carrie, there's something about me I haven't told you...I'm not like the other vampires." He shot me a serious look.

"I know sweetheart...I know your secret."

"You know?"

"Yes, you're an incubus or daywalker. Right?"

"How did you know?" He had a shocked look on his face.

"I did my research, love." I gave a little chuckle.

"So you know that biting me can change you as well? You can now become stronger than any one of us. You know that your desires for blood will now be doubled?"

That I hadn't seen or read during my research. I thought that the day walkers were calm and peaceful; I thought that they could control their desires. But how deeply mistaken was I.

Alex explained to me that only those born as day walkers posed such calm gentle nature. However, those who had bitten day walkers usually turned into savage, man-killing animals. Their thrust for blood usually controlled their behavior.

"So what are you telling me, Alex?"

"I'm telling you that you'll need to be really strong to fight these urges. You'll need to practice restraint...to find a way to quench your thirst without feeding off of humans."

"I can and I will." If there was one thing I was certain of, it was that I would kill myself before I went on any human killing spree.

"Okay, well...I will help you every step of the way sweetheart." His anger slowly disappeared, and he now had a pleasant look on his face.

He rolled over, pinning me to the bed, holding my wrists in his hands, stretching my arms above my head. He held me beneath him, using his weight to keep me immobile.

I was looking up at him with my clear green eyes, no hint of the deadly flat black he'd seen before. His lips came crashing down on mine with such passion and desire that my body ached to feel him within me once more. He pulled back suddenly, he sat back slowly, letting go of my wrists.

It was almost as if he was fighting a battle on the inside like he felt so remorseful that he couldn't go through with this.

"Alex, I feel fine. Perfectly normal. I do not want to attack you, or anyone else. I'm not particularly hungry for anything, blood or otherwise. I am more irritated at having you end our kiss." I gently poked Alex in the chest. "It's called teasing and that's not nice." I grinned up at Alex.

"There's a whole lot you don't know about me, Carrie. It's hard being like this, stuck in this body for eternity. This is a curse; don't think it's a good thing." His voice was cold and deadly.

"Wow...You sure know how to take away the fun in everything," I teased, trying to lighten up the mood. But he wasn't having it, he maintained a serious look. And so I wiggled out from under him and sat on the bed, facing him. "I know it's not going to be easy, but I have you right?" I reached out and touched his cheek.

"Yes, I'll always be here for you. You mean the world to me, sweetheart. I'm worried though. People will want to kill you because of this. Your father will be very upset. Have you even told him yet? There are only a few others like you, and they're all bad, evil beings. It's almost like a possession." Alex touched my cheek. "I'm so sorry for that. I never wanted to hurt you. You should have had a choice if you wanted to be changed or not. I took that away from you."

"Yes, you did. But you also gave me new life. I've never felt so alive before. I'm grateful to you for what you did."

Alex shook his head. "You think you'll like this but it's not fun. I know...I've walked down this path before. I know it's going to be the hardest thing you've ever had to do."

I could feel the tears welling up in my eyes, I was becoming emotional. This was not what I expected from Alex, I wanted him to be supportive. To tell me that he'd be with me no matter what. To tell me that everything was going to be alright. Instead, he made me terrified, scared of what I could become.

I quickly rose to my feet, filled with hurt and anger, and told him that I had to go. He tried to stop me but it was too late. I had already made up my mind. I would go home and tell my father the truth. And whatever happened I would simply have to deal with it. This was my curse to bear on my own.

"Let go of me, Alex! I need to leave now." He kept holding on to me, trying to console me.

"No! I'm leaving!" The more he tried to persuade me into staying the more irate I became. He'd spent all this time telling me how negative this life was, how bad I would become, but what I had really needed from him he hadn't provided. And so, now his words fell on deaf ears. I had heard all that I needed to hear.

"I know you think you're fine. But I think we should visit my Uncle James. He knows so much about this, and he'll be able to help. If anyone knows what you can do to help control your urges, it's him." He reached over and pulled me into his arms. "Can't you see I don't want anything to happen to you? I care a great deal about you. If something were to happen to you, I'd never be able to live with myself."

James was in his study. He welcomed Alex and me with a hug, as he led us to the chairs next to his fireplace. He listened patiently to Alex's detailed account of what had happened, his sharp eyes moving between me and Alex as we sat before him. When Alex had finished, James sat back in his chair, gazing into the flickering flames for a moment, deep in thought.

James leaned forward. "My, dear, what is your family background? Do you know where your people are from?"

I hesitated a bit before I told him exactly who I was: Carrie, daughter of Lamar, the vampire slayer.

James's eyes narrowed to Alex. "You brought Lamar's daughter here to me?" He sounded upset.

Alex scowled at James. "Is it necessary for you to speak like that to her?

"Yes, Alex. Because Lamar is ruthless and he'll have your head for turning his daughter. And besides, does your father even know about this? He'll be even more upset with you. You're in for a lot of trouble little boy. You both are playing with fire."

I was a little confused at this part. I didn't know if he meant Carrie's father or Alex's. If it was Carries, it should be reworded to be a little clearer. If it's Alex's, this would be a good time to bring up Charles and their background.

"Sir, I don't want to cause any confusion and I'm sure my father will understand, we just need your help. How do I control this hunger?" I interrupted his little rant.

"Uncle please, she's a good person. Don't judge her because of her father," Alex pleaded on my behalf.

"Well, isn't this funny? The daughter of the vampire slayer is now a vampire. And not just any vampire, but an incubus, and not even by birth." James let out a roar of laughter that made his fangs clearly visible to me.

"Yes and now she needs your help uncle. Please help us?"

James stood suddenly, pacing back and forth before the fire. "This is quite exciting. There is much more that makes what happened...or rather, what hasn't happened...to you epic."

"You're not making sense, uncle."

"I'm talking about the legend of the uprising. I knew that you'd probably be the one to stir this pot, Alex; never did I think it would play out this way. There is a battle coming up, and I hope you two are ready. In the meantime, I tried to control my hunger by feeding on cow blood, with a few drops of this in it." He walked over to the bookshelf on the wall and pulled out a book.

This battle is mentioned twice but never expanded upon.

I'm going to assume it's not the last battle in the story because it's not legendary at all. It keeps building up to something, but there's no payoff.

As he opened the book we soon realized that it was not actually a book, but instead some sort of case. He retrieved a small glass vile from it containing a green substance and handed it to me. "Metroid is an ancient potion that will help suppress your hunger. Two drops with every feeding and over time your craving for human blood will be no more."

I happily took the vile and thanked him profusely. "Don't thank me just yet, you haven't tasted it," he gave a light chuckle.

"It tastes awful," Alex laughed before telling me that he too had used this to suppress his hunger for human blood. However, he hadn't taken all of the substance in the vile and as a result, he still craved human blood from time to time.

We left James's house feeling a little more hopeful. I still had to go home and I still had to tell my father the truth about everything. And so, we headed out to my home.

When I got to my house, my father was already there. He'd been waiting for me inside when I got back with Alex.

"Where have you been, I thought you didn't feel well?" he asked with a look that let me know that he was not in a good mood. He didn't take the news well, in fact, he asked both myself and Alex to leave his house immediately.

Another instance that seems very rushed. She's spent most of the book worrying about telling her father and his reaction, and we don't even see it play out.

"Dad you are over-reacting. Please hear me out."

"Tell me something, did you want this to happen? Did you run into the arms of a vampire to spite me? Is this about not talking to you about your mother? Why would you do this to me?"

"To you? Dad this is my life...Mine!" I shot at him, as the tears streamed down my cheeks. I was so hurt that I couldn't even stand the sight of him anymore.

"Alex, let's go!" Alex, who had been silent the whole time, happily took the lead as we walked out of my father's house and life.

CHAPTER 6

I HAD MISSED my father dearly and decided to go back to him to ask his forgiveness. The last time we had spoken our conversation had been less than pleasant. He had practically disowned me, saying that he no longer had a daughter. When I went to my father, Alex came with me again. We were a couple whether my father wanted to accept it or not. The knock on his front door was light, I felt shyly timid as if he were a complete stranger. It has been months since we last saw each other.

"Carrie..." his voice was low as if he was sick. He did look older than he had when we last spoke. He seemed like he wasn't himself.

"Dad, are you okay?" I hugged my dad, and we remained in each other's arms for a brief minute.

"I'm so sorry Carrie; I should have never chased you away. Will you please forgive me, sweetheart?"

"No...no, I'm the one who's sorry. Will you please forgive me?" Again, we embraced each other.

I wanted to cry a cry of contentment. I was so happy to be back in my father's good graces.

"Come in, come in," he stepped to the side and with open arms as he invited us in. The place looked familiar like I hadn't been gone more than a day or two. As we followed him inside, I realized that he was definitely not himself. His movements were slow and cautious. This was quite the opposite of the man I had known to be my father, the agile man who always made hastened steps. A question soon surfaced in the back of my mind that made me wince a little. Now that he appeared to be so much slower, did that mean the end of his vampire-slaying days? My father's life revolved around his job, and him not be able to do what he did best would practically kill him.

He led us to the living room where he sat himself between Alex and me. At first, neither of us said anything, but finally, I spoke up. His behavior was oddly alarming. Once again, he assured me that all was well, saying that he was glad to have me home.

After probing him for answers, I finally got to the truth, the reason for his strange behavior. My father needed me, he needed Alex as well. Charles, his longtime vampire rival, had been gathering up an army of vampires to fight my father and his crew, and to rule the streets of Brooklyn. I couldn't quite understand why my father was now so fearful of Charles; he'd spent practically his entire life searching for him, trying to destroy him. And now, it seemed like the opportunity had finally presented itself, but my dad was shying away. I thought that my father would have been elated upon hearing such news, but instead, he was terrified.

"You don't understand, Carrie. Charles is stronger than ever, his army is larger than anything you've ever seen. He has been planning this for years now. Most of my best men are already dead, killed even before this war."

"What...What do you mean? What happened?" I leaned in closer to my father to hear exactly what he had to say.

"They were each attacked, during the day. Like how you were attacked at the bar. Your incident was just the beginning. Several other people have been killed since." He shook his head while closing his eyes trying his best to wipe away the painful memories that had been forever engraved in his mind forever.

"I'm so sorry dad." I leaned in closer, embracing him in an effort to console him. I had never seen my father in such a bad condition. It wasn't just his unruly appearance, everything from his head to his feet screamed unkempt neglect. He was clearly having a hard time dealing with all this loss.

In that moment, I felt horrible for my part in this whole ugly situation. I should have never left, even after we'd had our huge quarrel. I should have stayed home with my father, and over time, just as he'd accepted me now, he would have accepted me then. I apologized again, like a child who'd just been caught stealing from the cookie jar. But my father had already forgiven me and didn't want me to hold onto such hurt, such sadness.

"I'll kill Charles myself, if he lays a hand on you dad," I gnashed my teeth in anger.

All the while Alex sat there, silent. Charles was his father, but they'd never had a good relationship. In a way, Alex knew that a lot of the things Charles did were wrong, and he could never support that. Alex had explained to me what his relationship with his father had been, like a rotten apple almost; it couldn't be repaired or mended. They would forever remain a weird father-son pair. His father was a violent savage brute while he was a kind, compassionate, caring, loving young vampire. His mother had been a human because she chose to remain that way. That made Charles very angry, but he kept his word and never tried to change her without her consent. Recently she'd traveled overseas to stay in a monastery for a few days. She wanted to find her true self, to find her purpose in life. She'd spent all her life caring for other people, Alex and Charles, making everyone but herself happy. She'd become old and frail because of her unhappiness. Now she wanted more in life. She wanted to live a new life almost, a life where she lived for herself, not working to please everybody else. Alex was saddened by her leaving him behind, but he knew she had to do this for herself, for her sanity. And so he let her go.

This is huge! And definitely not a random "by the way" statement left for the end of the story. This goes along with the comments I made at the beginning of the story.

My father left us briefly and returned with a few of his men. There were about three of them in all. How would we ever win going up against Charles and his army of vampires? It seemed like we were about to fight an impossible war. As we sat at the huge round mahogany table, the eerie feeling in the room was apparent. We were like a group of people preparing our own funeral. We tried to draw up a plan that we could use to help defeat Charles. After hours of planning and preparation, we decided to call it a night. We would meet up tomorrow evening to finalize everything.

Tomorrow evening came almost too fast as we headed out to find Charles and his goons; we had one thing in mind – to fight till the end. Alex led us to his secret underground camp. As we slowly descended into the sewer one by one, the fear that was in the air was as real as the darkness of the night. The splash of the water almost startled us as our feet made contact with the water-filled ground. The only source of light that we had was the flashlights that we carried with us. Like a small group of soldiers secretly about to invade enemy territory, we walked in a straight line, as quietly and carefully as possible. The last thing we wanted was to alert Charles of our arrival. Our plan was simple; we had the element of surprise on our side. Charles would not know what hit him.

"Wait here," Alex whispered to us, as he ventured out further into the darkness. Unlike most of us, Alex had perfect nigh tvision, and didn't need a flashlight. We watched as he stealthily crept ahead of us. Before venturing out today, he'd informed us that Charles's underground fortress was like a death trap to invaders. He had booby traps all over, just waiting for curious lurkers who would dare try to break in.

"Come on," Alex signaled us with his hand. Without hesitation, we all followed, being extra careful as to not fall into one of the traps.

"Down that tunnel will lead us straight to Charles' quarters. The other alleys take you to different places in the city. That's how he gets around."

"We need to be very careful, especially now. Keep your eyes and ears open," my father encouraged as we continued.

In the distance, we could see a steel gate, perhaps leading directly to Charles.

"Is that what I think this is?" my father asked.

"Yes, but the gate is pretty well guarded by his night owls." Once again, Alex instructed us to stop.

The night owls, as they were called, were a group of highly skilled vampires, with the sole responsibility of guarding the gate that led to the head of their clan.

The tunnel was cold, just the way I had come to like the temperature. I no longer craved for the warmth of the sun, but instead, the cold of the night was much more pleasing to me. We watched as Alex crept up to the gate. He spoke in a language that we didn't really understand, an ancient language that some vampires used to communicate amongst themselves. He'd promised to teach it to me someday since I was now one of them.

We couldn't see who it was that he spoke to but we knew that they were there, just the way he shifted his head from left to right as if speaking to several people at the same time.

I gripped firmly onto the knife that I always carried, attached to the side of my belt. If anything were to go wrong, I would definitely be prepared. My eyes perused my environment, looking to the sides and then behind us. I could sense that something was amiss. It seemed all too easy. Almost like a trap – a big one. Did Alex set us up? Did Charles know that we were coming? I had several questions flooding my mind all at the same time.

I looked to my father, who looked equally worried. It was like we both knew that something really bad was about to happen, but we couldn't tell exactly what it was.

"This doesn't feel right," he whispered to me, pulling out his pistol and loading it with several silver bullets.

The other two men followed suit, fearing for the worst. I had already retrieved my knife and had it close to me, prepared to attack anyone or anything that pounced upon us. I was never frightened of using my knife. In fact, I think I thoroughly enjoyed it. Nothing could replace the thrill of boring this blunt object deep into the flesh of a wicked, evil being. There was nothing so titillating to me...well except sex. Sex with Alex, no doubt. That was amazing, nothing could compare to the intimate times that we spent together, caressing each other's bodies, and consummating our love.

In that moment I realized just how much I loved Alex, and if, God forbid, that he did turn on us, the same amount of love that I had for him would be instantly transformed to hatred. Immense hatred, one that knew no bounds. I would go to the ends of the earth to make him pay for breaking my heart. That was if he did. However, I wanted to remain positive about everything. Perhaps Alex was just as innocent as any one of us. He was just trying to help. I couldn't imagine what it would feel like to go up against my father, knowing full well that at the end of it all he was going to be killed. If anything, I would defend my father no matter what. But here Alex was fighting for the greater good. Going up against his father.

Suddenly our worst fears were confirmed. A cage from the ceiling came down, trapping the group of us who waited for Alex.

Alex turned around, seemingly surprised. I could tell from his expression that he had no part in this. Out of the darkness behind us came a tall dark sturdy man. I recognized him from the patch on his left eye. He was Charles, the head vampire of the deadliest, most dreadful clan of vampires. He was also Alex's father. "Well, well, well... Lamar, I must give it to you. You managed to turn my own son against me. Kudos." Charles gave a sinister grin as he approached the cage where he had us locked up like savage beasts.

"Charles, come on. Be honest, you turned your son against you because of your greed. Your evil ways, lack of respect for humanity." My father stared him directly in the eye.

I've always had a great deal of respect for my father, and up until now, I never realized just how brave a man he was. He stared his enemy directly in the eye, despite the fact that he was in a bad place. He had no fear, and he spoke his mind, regardless of his present situation.

"Life can be so much easier for you Lamar. Join me. Even after all these years of you killing everyone I love, I still know that you're a good man, Lamar." Charles now spoke to my father as if he were willing to put all their differences aside if my father said "Yes" and joined him and his little army. It would have been a great offer, had Charles not been so wicked. Joining him would mean going against everything my father believed, everything he'd fought so hard to get. Charles cared about one person only: himself. He did what he wanted, whether it was wrong or right.

"Charles, I'll never join the likes of you. You hear me? Never!" With that, my father inhaled and took a deep breath, releasing it with some of his saliva.

I looked in shock; my father had just spat in Charles's face. Everyone looked in horror, even Charles. My father's action had been so unexpected that an immediate reaction was impossible.

Slowly Charles whipped the slimy salvia off his face, with a look of pure hatred in his eyes. "I try to be civil and you spit in my face?" he asked, giving my father a serious look as he spoke. His question didn't sound like much of a question, it sounded like a warning. A threat even.

"Let them out father," in the distance, Alex's voice was heard. I could see him approaching us; he had a confidence like none other. He looked as handsome and proud as a peacock as he strode toward the cage and his father.

"How dare you interrupt me when I'm speaking," Charles shot at him in an irate voice. It was very apparent that Alex and his father had a bad relationship. That father-son bond was not there. I could tell just by the way they looked at each other and spoke to each other.

"I said, let them go, Charles," Alex spoke with much more emphasis this time, calling his father by his first name as well.

The older man was becoming more and more upset as his son drew near. If he could have snatched his head from the distance, I'm sure he would have. "I'm not going to repeat myself, Alex, stay out of this...I'll deal with you later."

Alex continued walking toward his dad. When he got close enough a struggle ensued. Both Alex and his father carried long samurai swords, which they used as they fought each other. It was easy to tell that Charles was a much better fighter than Alex; he handled his sword swiftly.

The clanging noise made by the two swords every time they made contact rang through the darkness. They were both relentless, neither one wanted to give up.

As they continued fighting, I tried to find a way to get out of our captivity. However, I had to do this as quietly as possible; the last thing I wanted was to alert anyone.

Charles and his son continued battling each other, unaware of anything else happening around them. Finally, I managed to pick the locks that secured us into the cage. The doors came open, and we rushed out. Suddenly we were surrounded by a gang of blood-thirsty vampires. They were all followers of Charles. They attacked us from all angles, with their swords and knives in hand.

This entire section of fighting could be more descriptive – more action, more intensity.

"Get her!" one of the older men called out to a group of men standing next to him. I had managed to successfully fight off everyone who'd come my way. I looked over to my father who seemed to have his hands full. He was very strategic with his every move, a skilled fighter indeed. I had been trained for years with my father, mastering the various fighting techniques just as he did; I was now almost as skilled as he was.

The fighting between all of us continued until we were the only ones standing. I looked in the distance and I could see Alex and his father still in a heated battle. Finally, with one good blow, Charles brought his son down to his knees.

"Alex...NO!" I rushed to Alex and stabbed Charles from behind, burying my dagger deep down into his back. His body cringed as I drove the knife deeper into his flesh. He turned around in a fit of rage, mixed with hurt, and delivered a hard blow to me. My body flew across the space, hitting the wall on impact. Immediately, as if it were a chain reaction, Alex stabbed his father from the front using his sword. My knife was still penetrating his back when fell onto the ground.

He was dead, and Alex was filled with remorse. It was the hardest thing he'd had to do. He had looked his dad in the eyes while driving his sword through him. After seeing Charles meet his tragic end, the other surviving vampires in his clan were terrified. They scrambled away, too scared to even look back. I decided that it was time to go home. With my father and his two other men, I went home. Alex remained with his dead father. He wept loudly, his pain evident.

Defeating Charles didn't have the type of satisfaction that I thought I would get. I was more miserable now than then. It had been two days now and I hadn't heard from or seen Alex. Perhaps he was still mourning, I tried to convince myself. And after all, he'd killed his own father. After about a week of not hearing from him, I decided to go visit him.

I found Alex sitting in his backyard, just pondering. His

mind seemed as far away as another land; he didn't even realize that he was no longer alone. He looked unkempt, like he hadn't taken care of himself for the past few days.

A smile touched his face when he saw me, the solemn mood that he was in seemed to slowly disappear as we spoke to each other. We talked for hours about our feelings, our fears, our hopes and our emotions. Just as I had suspected, the grief that Alex felt had been immense. So immense that he'd isolated himself from everything and everyone, even me. His mother was still away, so he spent most of his days in his backyard thinking.

"Why couldn't I just be normal? I'd give anything to live a normal, happy life. You know the type of life, where you don't have to worry about this god-forsaken urge for blood."

He was ranting about not wanting to be a vampire; he wanted to be a human. In all my life, I'd never witnessed anything like this – a vampire, wishing he was human.

"You are special, sweetheart. Be happy that you have this blessing. You can live life the way most people dream. Do what you want, go where you want." I embraced him slowly as I spoke, trying to console him as much as I could. If I could take away his pain with a snap of my finger, I would have. He meant the world to me, and it was literally killing me to see him like this.

"I'm not special," he shot back, like an angry child. "You don't get it, do you? This is no blessing, this is a curse. You live for years upon years, doing the same routine. Nothing changes, nothing excites me anymore." His voice went low with sadness.

I felt myself taking offense to his words, although I wanted to be there, supporting him; he made what we had seem insignificant. "Nothing excites you anymore?" I asked to confirm what he'd just said.

"Nothing," he spoke again, with his head bent over. He hadn't even looked up to realize that I was being hurt by his words. I tried to coach myself into ignoring what he was saying. He was hurting and perhaps wasn't even thinking straight. But his words kept ringing in my ears, "Nothing excites me anymore."

"I never thought that losing my dad would feel like this. We weren't even that close. I guess somewhere deep down inside I wanted him to change. I wished he would be there for me, for my mother. She loved him so much. All these years she never got over him. How do I tell her, Carrie? How do I tell her that her son killed her lover? My father."

In that moment, all the hurt that I had been feeling, subsided. The man that I loved was hurting, hurting deep down within. There was so much more to this entire situation. I pictured myself in his mother's shoes; I would die before losing Alex. He meant the world to me.

"Everything's going to be okay, my love, I'm here for you. I want to share your pain, feel what you feel, so that I can help you heal. Your mother will understand. She knows that your father had done some bad things during his lifetime."

There was a brief moment of silence, and then Alex let out a loud cry. He wept in my arms, like a baby crying for his mother. He needed to do that. I knew he had to release all his pain in one way or the other. Slowly I blew gentle kisses along the nape of his neck, trying to take away his pain, replacing it with sweet pleasurable sensations.

Slowly I brought my lips to his and captured his attention with a deep kiss. He didn't resist me; instead, his tongue explored the insides of my mouth feverishly. His body yearned for more and I could tell from the way he moaned, as my tongue left his mouth and trailed downward to the nape of his neck.

Suddenly, he hoisted me up upon him. I wrapped my legs around his waist as we locked lips once again. I could feel him walking with me, stopping only when he got to a tree. As he pinned my body between his rock-hard torso and the tree bark, tiny sensations rocked through me. It felt like I was in a movie, or like a fantasy slowly darting toward becoming a reality.

His tongue left my lips as his hand viciously ripped at my top, exposing my gorgeous melon-shaped breasts. His warm lips soothed me from the inside out as he slowly caressed my hardened nipples one by one, his tongue flickering over their perky tips.

Tiny spasms shot through my body, starting from the top of my back, going down to my spine, and crashing down into my wetness. I could feel the throbbing of his shaft as he pressed harder and harder against my body. His free hand moved lightly over my other nipple, gently pulling and tugging on it. I let out a soft moan, begging him to release me from my pent-up desires.

As he braced me harder against the tree, he slipped his fingers into the coolness of my core. Slowly parting my moist folds with two of his fingers, he stroked me along my tender flesh. I closed my eyes, biting onto my lips as another moan escaped my lips.

"Oh God Alex, take me now..." I cried to him, as my sweet juices slowly trickled down my temple of delight.

Alex happily obliged, whipping out his huge cock, stroking it several times with his hand, bringing it to the degree of hardness that pleased both him and me.

"Fuck!" I shrieked, as his huge manhood penetrated my core without mercy.

Like a savage beast consumed by his desire, he began thrusting his shaft into my wetness with fury, repeatedly. The quiet night was filled with the sounds of our moaning and groaning as we explored our ecstatic blissful moment together. Over and over, he stretched me beyond my limits with his rock-hard cock. He had the longest shaft I'd ever seen; it penetrated me deep within, almost to the point where I wanted him to stop. It was a sweet, pleasurable yet painful experience.

"You like this, don't you?" his voice was gruff and husky as he drove his cock into me, with several hard upwards thrusts.

I lost all control and cried out for more. Gripping a portion of my hair, he increased his momentum, slamming his huge meat into my moist heat. I could feel my wetness coating his shaft, and it was driving him near the point of insanity. Clearly, he was enjoying our moment of pleasure. He let out several loud groans as he rammed his shaft harder and harder into me.

"OH ALEX!" I cried out, teetering closer and closer to my earth-shattering climax.

Suddenly, I felt the sharp pains as his fangs penetrated the flesh of the nape of my neck. I let out a loud squeal, closed my eyes tightly, and gave in to his sweet painful sensation. As he drew my blood slowly, waves of pleasure rushed through me. I surrendered my all to him, allowing him to do as he pleased. When he'd had enough of my blood, he brought his neck to my lips and encouraged me to bite him.

As I bit him, he let out a loud groan. This was our ultimate commitment to each other. Slowly I brought my blood-drenched lips to his and pulled him in slowly with an intense kiss. The taste of blood, my blood mixed together with his, was enthralling. Our tongues danced together in the ecstasy of the moment.

As we kissed, Alex began thrusting harder and faster into me, serving me with a series of long hard thrusts, coupled with shorter, quicker thrusts.

With a final mighty thrust and a loud powerful groan, Alex exploded his load of hot sweet cum inside me. I, too, gave in to my desires, letting out a loud ecstatic cry as I summited my earth-shattering climax.

Our juices collided as we both simmered at the moment. Slowly I could feel my body calming down as tiny spasms shot through my body. It took us both a few minutes to calm down. As we sat under the trees, the beautiful moonlight glistened down upon us.

I could see the difference in Alex; he had a more positive attitude. He gave me a loving smile as we enjoyed the beautiful starry night.

"I love you, Alex." I brought my lips to his and kissed him lightly.

"I love you too. I'm happy that you're here with me. Let's live our eternity together." He smiled a smile that made my heart almost thump out of my chest.

I was crazy in love with this man, or shall I say, vampire. Maybe it's not all bad when you play with danger, I thought to myself, as we locked lips once again.

ABOUT THE AUTHOR

Shala Breece is an emerging erotica author of many erotica kinks and sub-genres. Be sure to check out other books and leave a review if this story got you hot!

Visit my blog at Shala Breece Blog

Join my newsletter for exclusive Shala Breece Newsletter

Sign up for Free Stories from Xplicit Press Authors

Xplicit Press Author Updates

Like Xplicit Press on Facebook

Follow Xplicit Press on Twitter

Readers: I want to expand a few of the stories to see where the characters can be explored further. If there are any of the stories that you would like to read more about again, I'd love to hear from you!

Keep In Touch
Shala Breece
info@shalabreece.com